THE STORY OF
BLANCHE AND MARIE

Per Olov Enquist

The Story of
Blanche and Marie

TRANSLATED
FROM THE SWEDISH
BY

Tiina Nunnally

Harvill *Secker*
LONDON

Published by Harvill Secker, 2006

2 4 6 8 10 9 7 5 3

First published with the title *Boken om Blanche och Marie*
by Norstedts, Stockholm, 2004

First published in Great Britain in 2006 by
HARVILL SECKER
Random House
20 Vauxhall Bridge Road
London SW1V 2SA

Random House Australia (Pty) Limited
20 Alfred Street, Milsons Point, Sydney,
New South Wales 2061, Australia

Random House New Zealand Limited
18 Poland Road, Glenfield,
Auckland 10, New Zealand

Random House (Pty) Limited
Isle of Houghton, Corner of Boundary Road & Carse O'Gowrie,
Houghton 2198, South Africa

The Random House Group Limited Reg. No. 954009
www.randomhouse.co.uk

A CIP catalogue record for this book is available from the British Library

ISBN 9781843432333 (from Jan. 2007)
ISBN 1843432331

Papers used by Random House are natural, recyclable products made
from wood grown in sustainable forests; the manufacturing processes conform
to the environmental regulations of the country of origin

Printed and bound in Great Britain by William Clowes Ltd, Beccles, Suffolk

For Gunilla

Contents

The Story of
Blanche and Marie

The Yellow Book

I

The Song of the Amputee

1.

"Amor Omnia Vincit"—love conquers all—is what she had written on the cover of the brown file folder, the one that contains the three notebooks. Above is the label "BOOK OF QUESTIONS" in bold block letters. It was as if two attitudes were being tested: the one above, forceful, optimistic, and completely neutral; the one below, fragile, cautious, almost entreating. As if she wanted to say: This is the starting point, and it may be true; oh, if only it were true.

Love conquers all. Against a person's better judgment, but nevertheless. It almost breaks your heart to see that: *Oh, were it only true; oh, if only it were true.* Everything very deliberately objective and proper, until the tone shatters. One yellow book, one black—incomplete or censored—and one red. Together they form a Book of Questions that has to do with Blanche and Marie. Nothing more.

It has to be accepted.

Love conquers all, as a working hypothesis, or the innermost core of pain.

* * *

Two years after Marie Skłodowska Curie received her second Nobel Prize, this time in chemistry in 1911—and in conjunction with the fact that her lover, Paul Langevin, became reconciled with his wife Jeanne and with her blessing arranged a more permanent sexual relationship with his secretary— Marie suffered a not unexpected and yet difficult loss when her friend, Blanche Wittman, was found dead one morning in Marie's apartment in Paris.

She had tried to climb out of bed to reach her wooden box on wheels. She couldn't do it. And then she died.

The cause of death was never established, but those who came to get her body noted both the negligible length of her body and the fact that Marie Skłodowska Curie insisted on lifting the amputated torso into the coffin herself. Afterwards, in farewell, she sat on a chair next to the deceased, with one hand on the lid of the coffin, while the pallbearers were forced to wait an hour in the room next door. She refused to give any explanation, merely murmured *I'll never leave your side*.

But later the coffin was, in fact, carried out.

In the only printed obituary, the deceased Blanche Wittman was characterized as a "legendary phenomenon," and her role as Professor J. M. Charcot's medium was mentioned. She left behind three notebooks that were not discovered until the late 1930s, and they have never been published in their entirety.

Marie Curie does not mention her existence in her memoirs, just as she omits so much else.

I don't blame her.

2.

Besides, who knows whether Blanche Wittman would have even wished to be mentioned?

Yet as a paragraph in the history of medicine, she did achieve a certain fame after her death, although she is never mentioned in connection with Marie Curie, but always as "Charcot's medium." One paragraph laconically states that she ended her life as a "martyr" and "sacrifice" to the scientific research surrounding radium. After Charcot's death and the chaos that subsequently arose concerning the scientific approach to treatments at Salpêtrière Hospital, she worked for two years in the hospital's x-ray department as an assistant. From there she went to Marie Curie's laboratory where, several years later, the discovery of radium was made. Who could differentiate between the emission of deadly x-rays and deadly radium? One took over where the other left off.

The end result: a martyr and a torso.

Yet after Charcot's death in 1893 there was almost total silence. During the last years of her life she intended to write a book about love. There is no mention of this in her brief obituary. Merely "died without arms or legs"—which is not entirely correct. She had one remaining arm, the right one, with which she wrote until the very end.

Her book was never finished. All that remains today are three notebooks, each of which measures 30 x 22 centimeters and contains forty pages, placed together inside a brown folder, a Book of Questions, as she called it. The first notebook she titled "The Yellow Book," the second "The Black Book," and the third "The Red Book."

No colors on the covers. With this three-part book she was planning to tell a story about the nature of love. Yet that's not how it turned out. What remains is a story about Blanche and Marie. How many lives can you say that about? Everyone has a story, after all, but few are ever written down.

The puzzling title "Book of Questions" on the outside of the folder is quickly clarified with a simple explanation. She had apparently decided that each section should start off with a question. Then she would answer the question as rationally as possible. The questions should be of the "utmost importance."

What color was your first dress? What was your first telephone number? Occasionally an abrupt and peculiar deviation: **What could be read from my father's expression when he performed the abortion?** Or: **Who sat next to Charcot's coffin during the funeral procession?**

Always very concrete questions. At times they seem pointless, up until the instant when you're enticed to answer them yourself. Then it's like a game that suddenly becomes true and terrifying. It all depends on you. If you continue, all balance and control are upset, and the compass spins as it does at the North Pole. I've tried it. The question about the telephone number can be answered swiftly and succinctly: "Sjön 3, Hjoggböle." Then things get more difficult. It's when you try to explain the obvious that the answer becomes lengthy, and frightening. There's something menacing about her Book of Questions, tempting you to enter into what is forbidden, or to open a door to a dark room.

Concise questions, detailed answers without any real connection to the question.

She must have been afraid. That's how a person reacts.

The three notebooks, the yellow, the black, and the red, are what remain. All the rest, meaning the external framework, is a reconstruction.

Occasionally the answer is quite terse: you have to assume that she intends to elucidate the answer later, after she gathers her courage.

For example, one note simply starts off with the question: **When?**

The answer concerns her doctor and lover, Professor J. M. Charcot. She describes a brief incident. It has to do with their first meeting. The first time he saw her, she writes, was through a half-open door. She was in a room at Salpêtrière Hospital, as a patient. The doctor who was treating her, *and with perplexing thoroughness examined me in spite of the fact that I had not yet achieved the fame that was later bestowed on me,* was employed at Salpêtrière Hospital; his name was Jules Janet.

She is precise about the external details. Two rooms, an antechamber, perhaps a changing room. She had been admitted to Salpêtrière Hospital after a series of sojourns at other institutions for some complaint, although we don't know what it was; it's possible that it was the same complaint for which she was later treated by Charcot. Meaning hysteria. She doesn't say.

Blanche was putting her clothes back on after being examined.

That was when she saw Charcot passing by in the corridor. He turned around and looked at her. The distance was barely four meters. She knew that he had seen. She slowed down her movements so that she dressed very slowly. She had turned her face away, twisting her body slowly. One breast was partially uncovered. She was certain that he saw her.

It was then, she writes—as if she had been concealing what was decisive in the wealth of details— *"as if I were burned into him, like a branding iron on an animal."*

About her youth there is only vague information. But she was educated. The quote about the branding iron is from Racine.

Her name was Blanche Wittman. At her death she was 102 centimeters tall and weighed 42 kilos.

She was then a sort of torso, though with a head. The lower portion of her left leg, the right leg up to her hip, and her left arm had been amputated. That's why her height is described as negligible. Otherwise there was nothing aberrant about her. Earlier, before the amputations, she was characterized by everyone who saw her as very beautiful. For certain reasons she came to be observed by many people, including many who were capable of describing her, meaning writers. From an objective point of view, only one photograph exists, as well as a number of drawings of her. In addition to the famous painting in which she is seen only obliquely in profile.

But she is beautiful.

She died happy. That's her claim in the last notebook, The Red Book.

Her unusually short stature was not, in other words, something innate. After being committed to Salpêtrière Hospital in Paris for sixteen years—from 1878 to 1893—diagnosed with hysteria, she was suddenly healthy. At that time, hysteria was a common ailment among women; it was particularly common during those years and struck nearly ten thousand women, but after Professor Charcot's death, it ceased to be common.

Ceased in actuality. Or was given a different name.

After her years in Charcot's research department at Salpêtrière Hospital, she worked in the x-ray department at the hospital, meaning she was no longer being detained. And in 1897 she was hired by the Polish physicist Marie Skłodowska Curie as a laboratory assistant.

She characterizes her time as a hysteria patient at Salpêtrière as happy, followed by a period that was not happy. After that come the laboratory years with Madame Curie, which were once again entirely happy, with possible interruptions for the recurrent amputations.

She never complains about being cut.

In the Book of Questions she wants to tell her story, to summarize and compare her experiences, partially from the hysteria experiments at Salpêtrière Hospital, partially from the physical chemistry ones under the guidance of Madame Curie, *in order to create in this manner a healing portrait of the nature of love,* which she compared to the nature of radium radiation and hysteria.

Healing?

In much of the first section of the Book of Questions, nothing but objectivity and happiness.

3.

The facts about Blanche Wittman's amputations are as follows. They have nothing to do with her attempts to explain the nature of love.

On February 17, 1898, in the Paris laboratory of Marie Curie, the radioactive effect of a black, pitch-like ore that was treated and "cooked" in the laboratory, and known as pitchblende, was tested for the first time. It was mined in the vicinity of the Joachimsthal district near the border between Bohemia and the future, and eventually former, German Democratic Republic. Pitchblende had been used for several centuries as an additive in ceramic glazes to create artistically interesting nuances in color. Pitchblende was actually an important color component in the production of the famed Bohemian crystal. It contained, among other things, the element uranium, which was important in the glass industry.

In order to conduct the experiments with pitchblende and extract certain uranium components from this ore, enormous quantities were required, several tons. It was tedious and dirty work, and it was carried out in an abandoned carriage house next to Marie and Pierre Curie's laboratory in Paris.

It was there Blanche Wittman found employment.

On that day, February 17, 1898—the date is of some significance in the history of physics—Marie conducted the first successful experiments with pitchblende, and it was observed that a strong, peculiar, and thus-far unknown type of radiation could be detected. It had already been found that thorium, the metallic element discovered by the Swede Jöns Jacob Berzelius in 1829, had a stronger radioactive effect than uranium. Now it was found that pitchblende emitted radiation that was far stronger. Even stronger than pure uranium.

What this "radiation" actually was, and where it came from, still had to be investigated. Pitchblende, as Marie Curie assumed, must contain a special substance, as yet unknown and possessing unknown properties.

It was in this small laboratory that the discovery was made.

The laboratory was actually *an old wooden shed, an abandoned carriage house made of planks and with a glass-covered roof that was in such a state of disrepair that the rain constantly drenched the miserable shed, which the Medical School had long ago used as an autopsy theater, but which later had not been considered worthy of housing human or even animal cadavers. There was no floor, the ground was merely covered with a layer of asphalt, and the furnishings consisted of several ancient kitchen tables, a blackboard, and an old cast-iron stove with rusty pipes.* It was in these miserable premises that three years earlier they had received a message from a certain Professor Suess, and from the Austrian state, which owned the mines in St. Joachimsthal.

The message was that waste products of pitchblende could be vouchsafed them. It was here that they discovered radium.

Marie immediately wrote a report.

Her hands are still beautiful. Blanche describes her as *an incomparable beauty who was inexplicably captivated by the sorcery of research.* On July 18, 1898, the members of the Institut de France listened to a lecture by her friend and former mentor, Henri Becquerel, who incidentally later lent his name to a unit of radiation relating to the amount of nuclear decay per second, designed to measure, for example, radioactive contamination of reindeer meat in the interior of the Västerbotten region following Chernobyl. And he was able to report that Marie Curie and her husband Pierre, through their experiments with pitchblende, had found something new and previously unknown. The title of the article was: "On a New Radioactive Substance Present in Pitchblende."

This was the first time in history that the word "radioactive" was used.

Still no flapping of the wings of history, only slight confusion.

The announcement in Becquerel's lecture was that a new substance had now been found that was 400 times more active than uranium, and that it contained a "metal," perhaps an element, that was not previously known and that possessed remarkable radioactive properties.

By the end of the year, this substance had been given a name. They called it radium. The substance had unusual properties. As they were able to achieve higher grades of concentration, they also found that the substance was spontaneously luminescent.

This word "luminescent" recurs in Blanche's Book of Questions.

Her text takes on an almost poetic quality. *Sometimes when I was praised during my performances at Salpêtrière Hospital, they would use the term "luminescent" about the impression that I made. Little did I know back then that this word, as if conjured forth once again by the magic wand of fate, would return in the world of physics and science, where I would now make my contribution by explaining the connection between radium, death, art, and love.*

Radium, death, art, and love. She has no idea what she's talking about. But it's probably the only way to say it. How else?

Death and beauty were perhaps very close to each other. She must be forgiven.

Marie, writes Blanche, often used to walk from her home to the laboratory on rue Lhomond in order to *inspect her domain.* Blanche—at that time not yet amputated—used to meet her on these "secret" visits to the laboratory.

She writes that *our dear products, for which we had no cupboard, stood lined up on tables and benches. From every direction we could see their faintly luminescent contours, and this shimmering glow, which seemed to be floating freely in the dark, aroused in us renewed excitement and enchantment each time.*

This is Blanche writing. We take note of the term "our" dear products. Yet she is only an assistant.

She later writes, in response to the question **When did Marie become an artist?** that a great intimacy arose between her and Marie, almost a kind of love, a love that was strengthened in the presence of this experience of beauty, offered by the enigmatic and colorful radiance of the "Radium." In her eyes the door was opened to a new and mysterious world, and in this world shimmering blue signals were sent out to the human being who was Blanche, and who at that time had not yet been cut.

She seems to have perceived these signals as a form of artwork. It was created by Marie. Not a word about Pierre.

In the Book of Questions there is also a short section that begins with the question **What is art in our modern times?**

She answers the question by giving a detailed and almost childishly enthusiastic portrait of the Universal Exposition in Paris in 1900. The text is filled with admiration for the emerging century's revolutionary scientific *advances*, those *giddy experiences and possibilities.* Knowledge that she had acquired from Marie, with the emphasis on radium.

That's why she devotes a great deal of time to the Physics Congress, part of the world exposition.

Around the Eiffel Tower a number of pavilions had been set up: one was a palace of electricity, where the *magic fluid* (!) called electricity was displayed. *There science and art were united.* One particular attraction was the American dancer Loie Fuller, who danced in a specially designed magic house, in a room illuminated by electrical beams colored by interchangeable filters. A moving sidewalk, driven by electricity, conveyed the spectators from one place to the next. You might say that electricity illuminated this breakthrough of modernity. She writes about all this in a solemn tone of voice.

But there was something else far more fascinating that drew researchers to the world exposition.

It was the newly discovered substance radium, and radioactivity. Blanche writes that researchers from all over the world came to Paris, and they came to consult Marie and her husband and co-worker Pierre Curie. *The watchword of the day was radioactivity.* Everyone was asking questions about what it was, these *colored messages from an invisible world*, which some still called "Becquerel rays," and which behaved so irrationally; they could sometimes be deflected with a magnet, sometimes not. A type of fluid, some said, and again began talking about Mesmer. Yet this seemed to be something different, like *a nighttime dream, the brief moment of awakening when the mysterious is still present yet seems real, and then quickly vanishes.*

These radioactive rays that perhaps had always existed in space and in reality! But no one had seen them! *Perhaps Phaedra was speaking of them when she sensed that Hippolytus became burned into her, as if she were an animal and he a branding iron.*

That is the introduction to The Yellow Book. No explanation other than one that is meaninglessly poetic. The reference to Racine is again very surprising.

Over time the research dealing with uranium and radium began to change. But this was a breakthrough, *a stellar breakthrough* (!)—or perhaps an attack on the rationalism of the Enlightenment.

No one could comprehend what it was.

These rays could penetrate dense shields but were stopped by lead! It was known that they could color glass; after all, pitchblende had been coloring the beautiful Bohemian crystal for centuries! centuries! and now blue-shimmering nuances were created that could not be rationally interpreted.

There were many questions. Was it an element? This substance could, in any case, induce radioactivity in other substances. Blanche writes that day after day she had stood with Marie in the laboratory. She had followed Marie's measurements minute by minute and seen an almost transfigured smile come over her face: *and then I understood that all of space was colored by radioactivity.*

That's how she sums it up. Three years of work with pitchblende, that dirty slag-heap of several tons, described as a metaphysical work of art on an afternoon in Paris.

Resplendent in the beauty of the new substance, she and her friend Marie had stepped through the door to modernity's twentieth century.

Marie Curie, or "Maria," as Blanche sometimes calls her in the Book of Questions, once took her by the hand, stood quite still, and spoke to her, or to herself. *I don't understand,* Marie had said, *I don't understand the capriciousness of this radiation. It occurs spontaneously, as if I were looking at the surface of the ocean, and there saw something start to move, rise up, as if the sea were a living creature, a marine animal or a living flower, and I watched the petals stretch out toward me, and it seems to me that this radioactivity breaks the first law of thermodynamics. What is the origin, the source, of this power?*

The radiation's spontaneous occurrence, she had told Blanche—her still beautiful and not yet amputated laboratory assistant, whose past and career as a medium at Salpêtrière had fascinated her from the very beginning—is a deeply puzzling mystery. Blanche had added: like love! But Marie had then turned to her with an inquisitive smile that was abruptly extinguished, as if she were at first uncertain before this peculiar image, then wanted to express disapproval. *Perhaps*, thought Blanche, *because she, as a scientist, disapproved of all poetic metaphors and was not yet prepared to take the step into the heartrending and ravaging world of art.*

That's how they conversed, that's how the remnants of their conversations are mirrored in the Book of Questions. This is before Blanche Wittman began her unsuccessful project to present the scientific and at the same time sensual explanation for the intrinsic nature of love. That was how Marie Curie still thought and reflected before she, much later, was imbued with a different insight through Blanche, and through the Book of Questions. An insight by which she was also captivated through her interest in Blanche Wittman's love relationship with Professor Charcot, her friend's alleged murder of the same, and her attempt to achieve a love that did not turn toward death and destruction.

Love conquers all.

One year later Blanche fell ill for the first time. It was inexplicable. The cost of the first operation was her right foot.

That was how it began.

But Blanche Wittman would long remember that Sunday afternoon when she and Marie, two beautiful women alone in the laboratory, hand in hand before the inexplicable miracle, were engulfed by the mysterious colors and radiance which, without them being aware of it, would shape the entrance of modernity into the museum of love, which was the still utterly perfect bodies of these two women.

4.

Today everyone knows, of course.

Both Blanche and Marie would, of course, die from these mysterious, beautiful, and enticing rays of radium. The ones that shone so enigmatically, but were the discovery which, like a door opening onto a black, menacing room, would change the history of the world.

First Blanche. Then Marie.

For a long time people tried not to see anything, and it was all concealed.

Laboratory workers died in inexplicably large numbers, most from leukemia; many were cut, as Blanche was. Yet this radiation was long considered to be curative. The radioactive health spas were very popular; the radioactive bottles of "Curie Hair Water," which was supposed to counteract hair loss, were sold in great quantities. A "Crema Activa" promised "miracles." A European pharmacopoeia from 1929 included eighty patent medicines with radioactive ingredients, all of them miraculous: bath salts, liniments, suppositories, toothpaste, and chocolate pralines.

By 1925, however, the picture had begun to change. That year Marguerite Carlough, a young woman who worked as a colorist in an alarm-clock factory in New Jersey, sued her employer, the U.S. Radium Corporation. She painted clock faces with luminescent paint.

Nine clock-face painters had already died, with serious lesions on their mouths as the first symptom. They were in the habit of moistening the tip of their brush with their own saliva, and after a relatively short time ulcerations, which were not luminescent in the least, began to appear. Their teeth crumbled away, their cheeks developed incurable sores, their tongues turned black. Gaping black mouths bore witness to the fact that the beautiful luminescent paint might contain a radiation that was deadly.

Others suffered from severe anemia, which was later called "radium necrosis." But the company that manufactured the beautifully painted clocks denied any connection, calling the symptoms "hysteria," which Blanche, known to posterity as "the queen of hysterics" might have regarded as humiliating, or perhaps an irony of history.

But she never found out about this; by then she was long dead. This was later. Yet it's an explanation for why Blanche eventually lost the lower portion of her legs and her left arm. The story she wanted to tell, which has to do with Marie Curie, and to some extent Jane Avril, but in particular Blanche and Professor Charcot—those four—has nothing to do with her poisoning, or even with Marie's much slower poisoning and death. Something else is the impetus for her Book of Questions.

It might also be said: the point of view from which we regard this account is a torso.

I can imagine that Marie felt a certain responsibility for her.

That was why she allowed Blanche to live in her home, protected her, talked to her, listened to her writings, read her Book of Questions. At least that's what I believed at first. But gradually it became clear: there were other reasons why Madame Marie Skłodowska Curie, twice a Nobel Prize winner, in both chemistry and physics, took an interest in this woman.

Blanche had led a remarkable life, after all.

She claimed to have killed Jean Martin Charcot, the world-famous doctor, whom she loved. She said she had committed the murder out of love, and thereby wished to blaze a trail for Marie as well, not by encouraging another murder, but by showing the way to a complete and scientific understanding of the nature of love.

Sorcery!

5.

It hurts to stand up on your own legs and walk.

Charcot once displayed her to Herr Strindberg. This is the only Swedish connection I could find to Blanche and Charcot. The experiments with hysteria cases at Salpêtrière Hospital were open to the public, after all, even though the "public" at first consisted only of a carefully selected group with scientific interests.

Later it included others.

Then came the performances at the Auditorium. The subject under scientific scrutiny was not a particular woman but rather Woman, and her nature.

Rumors of the experiments had spread among the intellectuals in Paris, and the rumors said—this was in the autumn of 1886—that certain experiments were now being conducted that showed Woman "in a certain sense was to be regarded as a machine, that certain emotions could be evoked through mechanical influences, so that by pressing on specific points, ingeniously devised, the evocation of an emotional prolapse could be produced. These emotions could not only be evoked, they could be repeatedly induced so that the hysterical and convulsive attacks thereby proved that Woman, precisely through her flight into hysteria and her scientifically monitored withdrawal from it, could be understood, the signs deciphered and examined."

For the first time it was possible to map the dark and unknown continent of Woman, in the same way that explorers such as Stanley! had mapped sections of Africa.

The image of the geographical explorer keeps recurring.

Then the rumor had spread, fortified in a certain sense by the fact that these women *in their hysterical state displayed a nakedness, although this was scientifically motivated and not to be compared with indecency.*

It was also in this way that interest among the general public developed.

The rumor was not entirely truthful. As his supporters pointed out, Charcot certainly did not believe that Woman was merely a machine, with pressure points, but that the interior of a human being could be visited! through this mechanical means of observation! like a descent into Snæffels volcano! a tunnel leading down! as the famed scientist Jules Verne had demonstrated! Maybe he was an author. But why these rigid boundaries between art and science? The center of the earth resembled the center of a human being! That's how it was.

The experiments were only the first stage in a longer, more dangerous expedition into the dark mystery that was the center of the human being.

Professor Charcot was not naïve. He was being scrutinized. Such enlightened men cannot permit themselves naïveté.

The experiments were open to the public to a certain extent. Blanche had been told that the notorious but interesting Herr Strindberg was to be present, and she had also taken note of him.

He was standing in the very back, looking curious but skeptical.

She ignored him. After the performance he did not approach to thank her or to speak to her. For that reason she had almost forgotten him, at least until someone reported that she and the experiment had made such a strong impression on him that that they later colored, or rather stained, a couple of his plays.

One was called *Crime and Crimes* and the other was called *Inferno*. No.

She had forgotten the titles.

Charcot's assistant, Sigmund, who was German or Austrian,

was especially excited because he considered this Swedish author to be very important, almost like Ibsen, the second greatest of the Scandinavian writers. Like him, Strindberg was intensely preoccupied with studies of the nature of Woman, and of love. The German or Austrian assistant had, however, pointed out to Blanche that in a certain sense Ibsen had always regarded love as a power game, which made him a competent but basically uninteresting artist, practically a political writer. While Herr Strindberg, who was apparently in many ways unbalanced, could often devise more interesting dialogue on this subject than the Norwegian.

Why? Blanche had asked.

Because of his terror of Woman, and his insight that she is an unexplored landscape where one must seek the unknown point in the great story of humanity from which what is terrifying and inexplicable becomes logical, Sigmund had replied.

The experiment had been quite successful. Herr Strindberg was almost invisible among the spectators.

Blanche had achieved with ease the third catatonic state, which was then invoked again. When it was over, she studied the audience, and Herr Strindberg in particular. *For several moments I observed that his lips seemed to part breathlessly, and that his gaze was no longer piercing, and yet it did not express sympathy for me, a little sister in the direst need. I was suddenly reminded of my brother, whom I otherwise never think about, cut off as he is from my love and my memory.*

That was the only time that Blanche came in direct contact with a Swede, or with any Scandinavian, for that matter, but it may have affected her view of northerners in connection with the events surrounding Marie's second Nobel prize and the Swedes' attempt to rescind the prize, because of love.

6.

From the Book of Questions it's apparent that by the age of sixteen Blanche had already been impregnated.

Her father, an apothecary who was in many ways fond of his daughter, then performed at her urgent request an abortion on his daughter.

When he inserted the instrument into her, he began humming a tune that she thought came from Verdi.

That's when she grew frightened, because she realized that her father, who only in a certain sense was responsible for the situation and finally was forced to give in to her *tearful pleas and appeals to his paternal feelings*, was also desperately terrified. Yet it was a different sort of terror from Herr Strindberg's.

Otherwise very sparse information about her father.

And Blanche left no children of her own. The year before she was admitted to Salpêtrière Hospital, and in between sojourns at a couple of other asylums, she returned for the first time in many years to her childhood home because her father was on his deathbed. He was gaunt and sallow and *formerly born in London*, a peculiar linguistic expression. He wanted her to sit on a chair next to his sickbed and keep vigil. When he asked her to do this, she stood up angrily and left the room, not returning until the following day.

Why? he then asked her. She gave no reply.

She brought some blankets, put them on the floor next to his bed, and went to sleep. Are you there? he called. She gave no reply. I know you're there, he repeated an hour later. She didn't reply. If you love me, my daughter, release me from this torment; close my mouth and my nose and put an end to my suffering. The next night she sat on a chair and watched his death throes. I knew you would come, he whispered. Why? she asked. Because you love me and can't stay away; now I'm begging you.

Then she placed her hand over his mouth and did not take it away until he had nearly suffocated.

Why? she asked. He did not reply, because he was afraid of her.

Don't be afraid, she then said, but I have to know why. He shook his head. Again she placed her hand over his mouth and stopped his respiratory passages. When she removed her hand, it was too late. She thought she saw a faint but triumphant smile on his just departed countenance. Why? she asked, furious and in despair; but it was too late.

In the Book of Questions one of the chapters starts with the question **Why?** Yet only her brother's description of her father's death is recounted, utterly devoid of any drama and without in any way intimating her personal involvement in his death throes.

Nothing more about the brother, except for a few quite transparent evasions.

About Blanche's mother a rather more detailed account.

It begins with the obligatory question, this time **When did I see my mother for the last time?** And the answer starts in an almost biblical tone: *When I was a child, spoke like a child, and had childish thoughts, and unlike now saw clearly, my mother passed away.* It then continues in a more normal tone of voice. The *I* who is speaking is Blanche herself.

I was fifteen, she writes, *and my brother was sixteen; even back then my name was Blanche, but they called me Ota. No one knew why. But when I turned sixteen and people started to be afraid of me, I decided that my name should be Blanche; and no one dared defy me. My mother died of love's desire and liver cancer, as I usually say in jest. She was unusually petite, only 150 centimeters tall, about the same height that I am now slowly approaching. No doubt Sigmund would have claimed that I always wanted to take after my mother. And now I'm approaching her; after the next amputation, I will pass her. She had dark eyes and used to whisper* cara, cara, cara. *My mother was a Corsican. I don't remember my brother.*

My left hand, which is no longer there, doesn't hurt anymore, but it can remember caresses. I usually think of this as the opposite of phantom pains and call it phantom love. It not only remembers caresses but also skin that it has caressed. A hand dispenses caresses, but it's also a recipient. I once mentioned this to Professor Charcot. He stared at me for a long time as if confronted by an accusation. Now the hand is gone, but not the memory.

Another term for it is phantom desire, but I choose to call it phantom love.

Whatever has been severed or has vanished also possesses its love, its memories. Maybe it's even possible to describe this phantom love. I can't estimate my mother's weight, but I do remember her hand, and her skin. It's natural for me not to remember my brother; he has been amputated, like my left hand and the lower part of my left leg, and yet the memory of him, what has been cut off, emits no signals of pain or love.

My mother died one summer when a great heat wave descended on Paris. It took three days before one of my paternal uncles could find a wagon to carry her to her home town of Sceaux, where she wished to be buried. She did not want to share a grave with my father, only wanted to be buried with him if he were still alive at the time, as she, with her terrifying kind of love, expressed it on her deathbed. I was the only one who wanted to accompany my uncle in her funeral procession. She smelled bad.

It was the sweet stench of my mother, the Corsican woman who did not wish to share a resting place with my father in the grave unless he were buried alive.

That was actually what she said. It could be interpreted in this way: that she imagined his desperate struggle to free himself from the confines of the coffin as retribution. We, my uncle and I, conveyed her in a wagon. It was the sweet stench of my mother that drove the horses forward at full speed.

Hoppla! *my uncle shouted merrily. I loved her.*

I chose to regard her remark about my father, suffocated inside a coffin, as a poetic image of their marriage, but when I said as much to her, she merely stared at me and declared that I knew nothing about love, at any rate, nor about poetry; the latter she added with a gentle and warm smile.

From her I learned not to regard factual events as metaphorical. Something is what it is. Nothing else. That was a useful lesson, which I also tried to convey to Marie.

At the ferry-station, at the crossing of the Cure River, the wagon seemed overwhelmed by grief and despair. The sweet stench of my mother's body caught up with the horses when the wagon halted to be loaded onto the ferry. The ferryboat draft animals were infected by the horses' understandable and natural fury, and for that reason the wagon, I mean our funeral procession, was marked by an almost panic-stricken haste while being loaded onto the ferry, and the wagon overturned.

The coffin floated out and slowly drifted to the middle of the river, where it sank.

Later I often used to imagine myself standing there on the river-bank, not weeping hysterically but completely calm, and I saw my petite mother in her coffin, surrounded by her sweet smell, vanish into the depths of the river, and I, the not yet full-grown woman, understood.

I write the word "imagine," and not "remember."

I understood that the sweet stench of grief, death, and love was diluted by this disappearance into the water, just as she was swallowed up by the deepest darkness of the river. Yet this became the phantom love that would endure for the rest of my life, more real than anything else, even though the real stench from my mother's body was diluted and then vanished, and in the end only the calm surface of the river remained as we all helplessly watched her disappear.

I am writing this as the answer to the question: when did I see my mother for the last time? It was on July 16, 1876, at four o'clock in the afternoon.

She disappeared into the river's embrace, as if she were swallowed up by the river's love.

And I remember that then, seized by a great sense of solemnity, I wished that one day, for the sake of my mother who was never allowed to experience love, I could write the definitive account about love, the one that is outwardly real, but also about phantom love.

That is the love reserved for the amputees, those reduced to a torso, which makes their task all the greater, the task of recollection and memory.

The instant that she disappeared (and therein lies the answer to my question), this story began. The one that contains the sweet stench of death. The rage against those who are alive. The lure of the desire that was denied her all her life, which I so wish she had been allowed to experience. Oh! I'm writing this with sorrow and despair; how I wish she had been allowed to experience what was denied her. But now there is only sorrow at the love she never experienced.

The person who wrote this was named Blanche Wittman.

She was a beautiful woman with a soft, almost childishly innocent face, a hint of dimples, and apparently very long dark hair. That is what can be discerned from the painting that exists, and from the sole photograph.

She resembles someone else.

Her story, briefly summarized, is as follows. At the age of eighteen she came to Salpêtrière Hospital in Paris and was admitted with nervous or, as was later established, hysterical symptoms. She had previously been treated elsewhere *staccato!* but she was now embraced by the Castle. Her melancholia manifested itself as *somnambular spasms*, that would, however, dissipate after a few hours. It was quickly ascertained that this was not a matter of any sort of epilepsy but rather hysteria. The hospital's director, a Professor Charcot—who later won fame as the first to diagnose and analyze various forms of sclerosis, including multiple sclerosis and certain neurasthenic illnesses ("Charcot's disease")—eventually developed a remarkable bond, bordering on devotion, to her, and she became his favorite patient.

She *assisted with the experiments on herself.*

At the time of their first meeting, Charcot was fifty-three years old. He used the term "experiment"; he did not think it was her talent for the theatrical interpretation of certain scientific problems that captivated him. He did not feel any desire for the women he put on display during his experiments with hysteria, which later included Jane Avril. He never admits, until his last trip to Morvan toward the end of his life, that he felt desire for Blanche. Yet in her Book of Questions she assumes this to be a self-evident fact.

He is not naïve. He describes himself as an enlightened man with a natural attraction to unexplored continents and a strong, rational belief in the inadequacy of reason.

In an article about Franz Anton Mesmer, Charcot acerbically pointed out the risk that an expedition leader might be betrayed, and he warned against naïveté. He was married and had three children. He also had another female patient who was his assistant and demonstration subject, a dancer by the name of Jane Avril. But after he met Blanche, Jane was "declared healthy," and she left the hospital after what was mistakenly described as a conflict between the two women.

Later she became famous as a model for the French painter Toulouse-Lautrec.

Charcot possessed the childlike nature of an explorer and a scholar. He was an adherent of the ideals of the Enlightenment, but he thought that inventors, researchers, physicists, and explorers should now be investigating new and mysterious landscapes. The female psyche was such a continent, not essentially different from the male, but more dangerous. Woman was the gateway, he writes, through which one must penetrate into the dark continent, which was richer and more enigmatic than the male. Jane Avril can be seen in many of Toulouse-Lautrec's best drawings: thin, dancing, occasionally with her face turned away but sometimes, most often, visible in a partial profile, like someone who has seen a great deal yet chooses to turn away.

With Blanche as the mute performer, the entry into the female and human psyche was staged before an audience of specially invited guests every Friday—later every Tuesday—at three o'clock.

Charcot had an Austrian assistant by the name of Sigmund.

His year with Charcot would color everything this man later did; his translations of Charcot's lectures are "spellbinding." Freud said that it was Charcot who changed his life.

He may also have meant Blanche.

In a certain sense Sigmund could never free himself from his expedition leader. Each of them thought that he had found the vantage point in the landscape from which the story could be regarded, and from there staged not only the nature of Woman but also of love, which was a religious rite, as well as a power play.

Of course other hysterics also performed at Charcot's demonstrations. But Blanche is the only one who is actually named. So why shouldn't Charcot himself have been branded! Like an animal!

In her youth, Blanche writes, she once read a French novel about a young Danish girl, twelve years old, who captivated King Christian IV of Denmark and made him dependent on her, *like a narcotic.* He was thought to be an alcoholic, but in reality he was merely enslaved by her! *Hoppla!* as Blanche's uncle had also once cried.

That *hoppla.* Like the wound from a burn.

This took place in the early 1600s. The Danish girl, who became queen, was at first young, then grew older, and in the end managed to annihilate her spouse, King Christian IV of

Denmark. He was captured by love. It was an execrable novel which asked the right question but failed to provide the answer.

At the end of the novel the question recurs: *Who can explain love? But what would we be if we didn't try?* She writes that she found this statement comical, but reassuring.

I don't understand her.

Right at the moment I don't like her, with her arrogance and harshness. It feels like a lump in my throat.

We're going to start soon, she keeps repeating, like a hope. Why not? This hope is the only thing that keeps us alive. I find a note on a scrap of paper; I must have written it and then forgotten. It says: *The Book of Questions is like a narcotic.*

Sorcery. Amor Omnia Vincit. How could she?

7.

I often wake up at night, unable to free myself. Perhaps that's her intention.

Blanche takes me by the hand and leads me downward. At first with coolness and innocence, until I'm calm. Later it gets worse.

No doubt that was how she wanted to help Marie too. Slowly, holding her hand, as her companion, down toward the center of the earth, onward to the final expedition, then out of the jungle, to the shore of the river, and that night in Morvan.

For Professor Charcot, the theatrical interpretations in front of the audience gradually took on an increasingly painful character.

He seemed to be exposing Blanche, yet he himself was exposed. The scientific diagrams of pressure points that were marked on the woman's body with a pen—the ones that would evoke attacks, twitching, melancholia, paralysis, or love—became at last so perfected and the results manifested by obedient clients were so successful, that he found himself very alone.

By then it was too late. He was in her power. In that sense she was similar to the young Danish queen, whose name she happened to have forgotten. For six years Blanche was the great theatrical star at Salpêtrière Hospital and in her way dominated the scientific entertainments of Paris in the same manner that Jane Avril dominated the Moulin Rouge.

Jane danced and was painted. It was called "The Fools' Dance," the dance she invented and created at Salpêtrière, the dance that bewitched everyone, although no one knew why.

One has to act the fool, Charcot had told her.

Jane was often seen but never painted until she left Salpêtrière and became world famous. On the other hand, there is only one artist's painting of Blanche. In it she is depicted as powerless.

Blanche killed her lover, Professor Charcot, in August 1893. A couple of years later she left the hospital, and in 1897 she took a position with the Polish physicist Marie Skłodowska Curie. Her first task was to work with pitchblende. The fact that this mineral emitted radium was unknown. She was forced to undergo amputations until in the end she was a torso.

It was during this period from the first amputation up until her death that she wrote the Book of Questions. This is the story of Blanche and Marie.

Marie Curie loved Blanche, even after she was transformed into a torso.

Marie also had a lover. He betrayed her, which put her second Nobel prize, the one for chemistry, in jeopardy. In her notes, which she called the Book of Questions, Blanche writes that in the midst of Marie's most difficult crisis—after Marie's return from England when she received word on the very day of her arrival that her lover had given up and found someone else—she described for the first time her final confrontation with Professor Charcot.

That was the first time Blanche told anyone about it. She writes that she did this to diminish Marie's naïveté, *to get her to stand up on her own legs and walk.*

The expression is a peculiar one for someone who was without legs, but it recurs.

She writes: *I explained to Marie, as she, dissolved in tears, sat next to my bed and caressed me with her right hand, which was crippled, almost eaten away by the hard work she had carried out with radium, I explained that I killed him because of his loyalty, and his childishness, and because he refused to stand up on his legs and walk, which is the mark of love. I have never met anyone that I loved as I loved him, no one; I loved him more than my own life, and that's why I forced myself to keep him away. How great love is, how difficult to capture, like a butterfly that has escaped from heaven. But in this age of great upheaval, which is the trademark of the new century, how can we find connections, if not through love?*

That's the whole story in a brief, untruthful outline.

8.

It's necessary to picture her as a child defending herself.

She writes terse statements that occasionally seem stylized, in which the words often contradict each other. Because she can't manage to make sense of it all, she dreams of a coherence that she calls "radium" or "love" or "the new century." I think she was a petite, kind-hearted, and not at all callous woman who found out too late what she was supposed to do.

I have never met a woman like Blanche, though I've met a

few who were on their way to becoming like her. They found themselves at a forbidden boundary and were frightened away, or they crossed it but that was the first time they ever stopped.

When I was a child, spoke like a child, and had childish thoughts—I admit that the phrase is hers—the gospel was a message of love, and all love was partly imposed, partly forbidden. It created a temptation that was explosive and therefore also deadly. Love and death were related; we could not free ourselves. Everyone talked about love, but no one explained it. It was also the greatest sin.

And so you can't give up.

If you don't give up, then it's possible to explain anything, even the pain when you finally stand up and walk. *Love cannot be explained. But what would we be if we didn't try?* These manic repetitions! But what was she supposed to write as she lay in her wooden box, as the cold crept farther and farther up toward her heart and everything rotted away?

Almost the same wording occurs five times in Blanche's Book of Questions. I read the words, and for a moment the world stood still while my heart kept beating and beating.

In reality she was just trying to tell a story.

No doubt we should be content with that. There is nothing more noble, as long as it's a story and not merely an evasion. I think of her as being something much simpler than she claimed to be.

She didn't intend to kill! In reality she was no doubt a very simple and nice girl from the country who got into trouble. I once knew someone like that.

Before I gave up and began to understand, I didn't like the fact that she wasn't a Swede. That she was a foreigner and spoke French. But that's how things were. What could I do? I suppose there is a little of France everywhere. Or a little of Paris, or a little of Poland. That shouldn't make any difference. I don't know why I'm apologizing, but no doubt I'm frightened. Nothing wrong with being frightened. Somewhere there's always a benefactor to turn to, and for Blanche there may have also been salvation and forgiveness.

Now it's going better. At first it was difficult to reconstruct her; now it's going better, even though it still hurts. At first there was a lump somewhere deep inside, but now it's starting to dissolve. I think that she, if she dared to be honest, should not have acted so cruelly. No doubt a person acts without pity only when believing that she herself will receive none.

When I was a child, talked like a child, and had childish thoughts, meaning when I was ten years old during the Second World War, I dreamed of someday falling in love with a blonde girl who was very beautiful and very loving, who was paralyzed, sat in a wheelchair, and played the violin. I have no idea where this idea came from. I had never even seen a movie. I assume that I first pictured Blanche in this way, as a modest, beautiful blonde who played the fiddle and was dependent on me to move. It was all quite natural. This was Blanche, after all. I recognized her. She had finally come back. It's necessary to reconstruct what she had been through because she herself said nothing. But there was no doubt it was her. It was the part about the torso and then this almost forgotten dream of the girl in the wheelchair with the violin.

Now it feels much better. The lump is gone. All those stories a person has read! The one about the girl with the red shoes! Or the one about the little mermaid! There was always something about enormous pain whenever they stood up and walked. Like knives piercing their feet.

Soon it will be all right again. The girl's name was Blanche. Amor Omnia Vincit.

I I

THE SONG OF THE RABBIT

1.

IN THE BOOK OF QUESTIONS BLANCHE CALLS HER THE RABBIT. It might be a contemptuous intimation of sexual licentiousness.

Perhaps the Rabbit is unimportant.

But if she's important for Blanche, then she's important.

Sorting through the cast of characters in the Book of Questions, only three women are found right from the beginning. They are Blanche, Marie, and the Rabbit. Later Hertha Ayrton appears, but that's close to the end. And Blanche never met her.

The Rabbit?

At first I thought that all of them were afraid and rather childish, afraid of not being able to withstand love. But that's probably wrong. It wasn't fear but innocence in the midst of the filth, which is what makes people at last stand up on their own legs and walk.

Occasionally in the Book of Questions it suddenly seems as if Blanche stops, there's an abrupt pause. It's possible to picture her looking up from her wooden box and peering out the window at the trees and the leaves, as if there were a riverbank beyond. Or maybe she glances down at the blanket wrapped around the stumps of her legs; she frowns, with that look of innocent surprise on her still childishly beautiful face, and then she always writes *I'll start soon.*

You get used to it, I ended up liking it. After all, she wants us to understand but she's a little frightened, can't comprehend why we don't understand! Why this holding back! Then this innocence and timidity; questioning whether she should continue, that must be it.

That must be why. That's the sort of thing a person writes only when not really daring, or having crossed a boundary in desperation. No one knows anything for certain about the six thousand women locked up at Salpêtrière Hospital, but they were there, all around her. *I'll start soon.* It has that undertone of childish terror, joy, and slight despair; I recognize it.

It's not difficult to understand that Blanche's hands and arms were affected by the radiation.

But her foot? And later her leg?

Maybe that was something else. There is so much about Blanche that might come under the phrase: *that was something else.*

So first there was Blanche. Then Jane Avril, whose real name was Jeanne Louise Beaudon.

She plays a very limited role in the story about Blanche, Marie, and Professor Charcot. But one afternoon in June (no year is given in the Book of Questions, but it's possible to surmise that it was around 1906) she appears unannounced to visit Blanche. This is the first of two visits.

The second takes place a month before Blanche's death. Marie, Blanche, and Jane, the three of them, sit on the terrace. Trees. Foliage.

This is the best meeting, quite unlike the first one; it's the very starting point, or the point from which it's possible to tell the story.

We always hope that such a point exists in every person's life. That's probably why we continue.

The first meeting is in the middle of the series of amputations—Blanche has been diminished by one arm and one foot, but she can walk with the help of crutches—and Jane is unperturbed and friendly. **What is the reason for Jane's visit, and who has told her about my condition?** That's the headline in the Book of Questions.

She brought with her a loaf of freshly baked bread, which, she explained, was garnished with raisins and Abyssinian nuts (?) and flavored with rosemary. She said that she wanted to share the bread with Blanche, along with a glass of wine, as a gesture of friendship, and talk about old memories.

She glanced around the room, as if only now discovering where she was. She noticed some of Marie's equipment: several glass retorts and flasks. She went over to the work table, bent over the notes with chemical formulas, and stated dryly: *So this is what they give the Nobel Prize for.*

"You have distinguished friends," she said. "You've come up in the world."

Come up? Blanche is not lying in her wooden box, though it has been constructed and stands next to her bed. But still!

Jane's clothes are *extravagant.*

That is the word used. She looks the same age as children wearing make-up who are tormented and yet patient. Blanche writes that she doesn't understand what this unusual guest with the loaf of bread signifies. That's why she starts off almost in panic, *with what for me is unusual nervousness,* to talk about Jane's great successes at the Moulin Rouge and the fame that has come to her through the illustrations done by the painter Toulouse-Lautrec, the ones in which Jane plays a charming and dominant role. But then Jane interrupts, brusque yet friendly, and asks almost solemnly:

"Blanche, how are you?"

"You can see for yourself."

"That's not something anyone has ever been able to see," replied Jane after a moment's silence. "You always had a terrifying strength; I've always been afraid of you. You were so unbelievably strong, everyone was afraid of you, don't you know that? I felt sorry for Charcot. He was so afraid of you."

"That's enough," Blanche whispered.

Jane sat down on a chair, silent. Time passed.

Then, almost in a whisper, she started speaking.

She wanted to talk about Salpêtrière, which was not merely a hell but something else, something very precious. She uses the word "precious." The precious part was something that she had lost, a memory that she was trying to recall. *Even in the deepest despair a moment can be found when anything seems possible,* something like that, *when you're free and can start over.* At times her voice almost vanishes.

"I've forgotten. There's nothing I can do anymore. Dear Blanche, I beg you, *the only thing I beg of you is to give me back a memory.*"

Blanche, puzzled by the sheer linguistic aspect of the phrase, then asks:

"A memory?"

"What it was like."

"Give it back to you?"

"Yes," Jane whispered, with the same insistently gentle despair, according to the Book of Questions. "It's been lost."

"What memory do you mean?" Blanche asked, putting down the piece of bread she had been given, *acting as if it had been poisoned, which I hope Jane noticed.*

"When I danced. And believed it was possible to start over."

"You've forgotten?"

"Why else would I be asking you?" replied Jane.

A long silence then ensued. Blanche writes that she now felt calmer, no longer caught off guard. She wrapped the blanket closer around her amputated body. *It was now time to launch a counterattack against this impudent intruder.*

"No, I don't remember," said Blanche. "And if you don't remember, you little bitch, then how am I supposed to remember?"

The appearance of the phrase "you little bitch" is very surprising.

"*La danse des Fous!!!*" said Jane Avril, pretending not to hear the vulgar insult, and acting as if her own outburst had not occurred and was of no concern. *I've forgotten, but I'm sure you remember 'The Fools' Dance' at Salpêtrière, the butterfly!*

That's where this section in the Book of Questions ends.

Whether or not the conversation has been accurately recorded, it's still remarkable. This is not how people express themselves, *as solemnly as a corset,* as she says somewhere else. And that sudden hatred. It doesn't make sense. Yet later on, they would meet one more time, just before Blanche's death in 1913, together with Marie Curie.

On that occasion only silence, sorrow, and warmth.

But nothing more about the bread, about the memory of a lost moment, about "The Fools' Dance," about the ground-breaking performance that Blanche must have witnessed, though it was now nothing more than *a lost memory.* As if it were possible to amputate the memory, a phantom memory without pain, like Blanche's amputated limbs, but a memory that surely could be retrieved, like an object from history: yet in the end nothing was lost or without significance and meaning.

2.

Jane Avril was her stage name.

Her given name was Jeanne Louise Beaudon, and she was born on June 9, 1868, in a town called Belleville, which was actually a suburb of Paris. Her mother was a whore. Belleville is located on a plateau that is so high and so steep that it hardly seems connected to Paris. Later on a cable car was erected, descending from the plateau so as to improve the connection with the *city of light and joy*. Her mother's career as a whore lasted from her fourteenth year until she was thirty-one; after that she was too fat and had to make her living telling fortunes by reading coffee grounds. Her mother called herself a milliner. "My mother was very beautiful, a brilliant and celebrated Parisian during the second empire," writes Jane in her memoirs, published in the 1930s. She also intimates that her father was an Italian count, which is something anyone can claim; in most cases it's even plausible. *My father was an Italian count*, but he may have been, more credibly, a local farmer by the name of Fant. That's why her mother took the title of "Elise, Countess of Font," and left the care of her child to her parents. This was during the siege of Paris in 1870, the same year that Charcot sent his family and children to London. I will return to this.

Jane is adopted as the mascot of a group of Prussian soldiers, and the first German sentence she learns to say is: "All Prussians are swine," which arouses great merriment.

Eventually her mother takes her back and abuses her, with intervals of respite spent with her maternal grandparents, with whom she has a pleasant life. But one of her mother's former lovers takes pity on Jane, and she begins to fill out, which he appreciates in both a spiritual and carnal sense.

Jane is clever; she knows how to "clean house, light a fire, and cook." She's a little imp—that's the general opinion—though demure. "Never forget that you're the daughter of an Italian count," her mother constantly admonishes her. During the first part of her life, Jane believes in God and wants to save her mother from eternal damnation; later she gives it up, including her attempts to save her mother.

Jane's early biography is dreary.

By the age of thirteen she's a beggar at the marketplaces in outlying districts. A certain sentimentality, typical of the times, hovers over her youth; it's only later that she becomes famous and brimming with talent, and then chiefly through the paintings of Toulouse-Lautrec.

She plods unremarkably through her early years.

Suddenly she starts having convulsions, accompanied by involuntary movements. The first time this happens, the convulsions are thought to be associated with her feelings of guilt. She was reluctant to massage one of her mother's benefactors who had suddenly been seized with pains in his back. Her sullen but at the same time childish defiance had provoked the fury of her mother, who had then beat her. When her mother's friend again demanded help in his situation that was almost like an illness, the girl refused, in spite of being rebuked, although she shed no tears but merely resolutely contorted her face. That's when the girl's defiant attitude, in some sort of medically indeterminate way, was transmitted to her limbs, and a condition resembling dancing which both astonished and frightened those present, meaning the ill mother and her benefactor. The girl's illness was labeled dancing sickness or St. Vitus's dance.

That's how it started, so innocently and at the same time mysteriously.

One of her older lovers and protectors, a Doctor Magnan, was a psychiatrist who had learned to appreciate the young Jane chiefly during her leaner and more childish periods. And he sees to it that she is admitted to Salpêtrière Hospital, under the care

of Professor Charcot in department two, section three, on
December 28, 1882.

3.

How could she not remember that city within the city, the
one that was called Salpêtrière!

And it's there to this day.

She had always imagined heaven as a castle—not while she
was saved and was still trying to save her whoring mother from
hell, no; but somewhat later after she had given up—a castle
with walls protecting it from the world. It was up there that she
would someday be taken, released from her little whore of a
mother and the benefactors among her mother's customers, the
ones who preferred her and her more childish figure, as opposed
to her mother's stout and flabby body. Or perhaps she had imagined heaven as somewhere on earth! The way one of her benefactors once recounted to her. He had called himself a man of
the Enlightenment! He had told her that this heaven was to be
found on earth, nowhere else. And in her childish way she had
then taken the fiction further, had imagined that "heaven"
meant that these benefactors would be flung away from her
mother; that her mother would be transformed, become softer,
gentler, and slow in her movements, not quick and hard in that
disapproving way that hurt and left painful bruises on the young
girl's body; that an angelic transformation of her mother would
occur in this earthly heaven.

That's how she imagined the enlightened heaven would
look, but what Jane now entered was merely the heavenly castle
by the name of Salpêtrière.

Salpêtrière was in fact a castle in Paris, a Castle! And that's
where the women gathered who were confused by love. Those
who were morally degenerate, those who were aging, and those
who would soon find love, but had collapsed during the wait-

ing. This is what they had in common: love had played a role for all of them, and they had been betrayed.

The hospital had 4,500 beds, but not everyone who was admitted could be offered a bed. The castle far exceeded its capacity. It was first and foremost an *"Old Folks' Home,"* but it was also a warehouse for those who were left over. That's where the *leftover* women were taken who no longer had benefactors or guardian angels. But it was not the aged, the demented, or the insane who were the foremost clients in this black castle in the middle of Paris. The old people (who were all women because during this period men were not admitted) were certainly in the majority, but they were not the ones who formed the pulsing and mysterious heart of the Castle. No, as Jane Avril later writes in her memoirs, it was *the mentally retarded epileptics and the hysterics who formed the upper class in this mournful hell, the ones who were famous. They were the envied upper class in this tragic and comic collection of six thousand gray shadows who, muttering, shrieking, or sobbing, moved like slow-moving toads through the filthy passageways and rooms between the meter-thick walls or out in the open courtyards in irresolute groups.* The words suddenly seem almost eloquently vivid in Jane Avril's otherwise thoroughly opaque autobiography.

A hundred years ago.

That's where they were taken, Blanche and Jane and the *six thousand other flesh-and-blood shadows* who thought they were still human beings.

The army of shadows is gone, but the Castle is still standing, with its walls and archways, and its library with the famous painting depicting Charcot and Blanche during a session. The painting! the famous one! how it's been interpreted! the altar painting of repressed eroticism! the holy grail of pietistic sensuality! the symbol of woman's helplessness in passion! such submissiveness!

Or merely a picture which, enticing and cold, is a memo-

rial sketch of an expedition that failed on its way to the continent of Woman and love.

It's there to this day.

The castle in Paris, now stripped of what Jane Avril saw
when she was brought inside that Labyrinth inhabited by
human rats. The image of the *lunatic women's castle* recurs in all
the descriptions; it's enticing and repugnant and lacks any connection with us, we say: like a dark dream just before a brighter
awakening, which is *the enticing image of Blanche in a swoon.*

And Professor Charcot practically in her arms, or she in his.

That's where Jane Avril landed, after completing her education under her mother's direction, after an exciting and unusual
upbringing, as yet a woman without talents, not yet world
famous as a model who dances.

Why was she called the Rabbit?

No, that was not why she was called the Rabbit.

It might otherwise be used as an image of pietism's sexuality, which was far removed from Jane Avril but perhaps closer to
Charcot, if I know him right; and why shouldn't I know him
when Blanche thought that she knew him?

What right does she have!

What right does she, of all people, have to comment on
pietism's repressed sexuality? None! None! When the World
War, the second one, reached the small villages along the coast
of Västerbotten, everyone was exhorted to acquire rabbits. The
idea was that they would be kept as reserve provisions if war
actually arrived. They swarmed around in their little cages, and
the children, those who had all the secret and dirty instincts of
a child, all of those basically sinful and pious children watched
the rabbits copulating, constantly! constantly!

And since sexuality was the most forbidden thing, it was
with horror that the supervisors and benefactors later, much too

late! discovered that the children—who were, like myself, products of pious pietism's fixation on forbidden passion and on Woman, she who was, after all, the innermost driving force of sin and the one who created temptations, the ominous end station of sin—all these innocent children would lie in small heaps in meadowy glades or in the forest or in the snow and, fully dressed, perform the daily convulsive motions of the rabbits when they copulated, in groveling, rippling heaps.

As if sexuality had bubbled up beneath the ice cap of piety, and had become irresistible.

For these children the village had become a kind of lecherous limbo, innocently created by these humping, rubbing children beyond the reach of the Christian message of love, which was also the law that sexuality was the most forbidden thing and thus the enticing boundary that the humping little children, concealed by their rabbit games, wanted to approach.

Jane was forced into prostitution at the age of eleven. Blanche was never a prostitute. At first she loved Jane; later she feared her. By the time she saw her again, it was too late.

But those amputated passions! What power!

There's no reason to apologize for the twentieth century. Why should apologies be made for a century that was not able to choose its own roots?

Ridiculous.

Yet even little villages along the coast of Västerbotten were no different. We were all fundamentally Moravians. Ridiculous to apologize or feel ashamed about the roots of sexuality. Even as late as the mid-1700s, when Moravians in Bohemia held a wedding, the couple was led to the blue room, where their first intercourse was supposed to take place under the eye of an elder of the congregation. Back then the act was ritualized, like a church service. The bridegroom was supposed to sit on the floor with his legs stretched out, and the woman would sit astride him.

Then the deflowering would be carried out, with an elder of the congregation sitting on a chair against the wall.

What is the strongest driving force of faith if not desire!

4.

The Castle is still there.

Was it really a castle of passions? A seething saltpeter cauldron that even today has a mythical radiance? A magical castle which was once a laboratory that was supposed to investigate a secret more important than radium? And was it really inhabited by rats? A castle?

No, not likely.

At the very end of a series of archways there was an opening facing La Place Sainte-Claire which, in the midst of the degradation and accompanied by the plodding and shuffling sound of the human rats, opened onto space. If you crossed the square and then crossed rue de la Cuisine, which also happened to be open, you would come to the quarters of those suffering from nervous diseases, epilepsy, and hysteria. That was where the famous Professor Charcot ruled over these lewd and menacing women. The most extraordinary among them, those whose experiments attracted the greatest interest, were the women who were called hysterics and who urgently worked to become "stars among the rats." It was said that during Professor Charcot's performances and treatments they would seize every opportunity to attract attention through extravagant contortions, arcs-de-ciel, various acrobatic exercises, and guttural shrieks of despair, joy, or relief. These were the theatrical manifestations that were supposed to demonstrate the previously hidden pathway into the terrifying and repellent world of womanhood and love.

* * *

Just like us, the children in our little village, I sometimes think.

Did we ever grow up?

Jane, whose name at the time was still Jeanne Louise Beaudon, entered this women's castle without fear, thought about the life she had been leading, and gladly decided to amputate all memory of it.

She discovered that this heavenly refuge certainly did resemble a hell, yet a hell that was bearable and amusing. The women were exploited, but they never entirely surrendered. Her fellow patients spoke to her in a reassuring manner. They harbored no distrust, she writes, of "my small, slight, thin figure"; and she became familiar with the rules and escape routes of the institution.

The staff was eager to be of service and was cultivated by the female clients. The doctors were young; they carried out their examinations with scientific precision. And when the most favored of the women became pregnant, they were forced, to their great regret, to leave the hospital to give birth. But they always returned, *like lost lambs returning, at last, to the protective ewe.*

The Book of Questions contains none of this flowery language. A few isolated questions regarding Jane Avril, and in one place a most enigmatic answer. The question: **What did he see in Jane?** And the answer: *He loved animals as he did himself, and there were times when I felt a jealousy, almost a hatred, toward those helpless creatures who swallowed up so much of his love.*

That's all. That's the whole answer.

Love can arise when a person shares his darkness with his beloved. Does hatred also arise then?

5.

Blanche Wittman was the obvious authority for Jane to consult when she came up with the idea for the great dance performance to pay homage to the fools.

Blanche had influence, after all. She was the queen of the hysterics! Rumor had it that Professor Charcot was in love with her and that she had great power, though she refused to allow Professor Charcot admittance to her *innermost gardens*.

The women who were particularly favored by Charcot, those who more or less regularly participated in the medical experiments and were the chief subjects at the scientific and public analyses, were housed in the great Duchesse de Boulogne Hall, on the ground floor.

The women who were insignificant or worn-out hysterics were housed on the upper floor. They included the ones who were considered less aesthetic, those whose attacks seldom manifested themselves in a scientific manner and who were confined at Salpêtrière for such a long time that they gradually lost their minds and sank into apathy.

Jane was still a child, though she had a fourteen-year-old's charm. At the same time, she possessed a child's cruelty and curiosity, and she loved to provoke the patients whom she found comical or repulsive. One of them was a tall, majestic woman with close-cropped hair as white as snow. She was called La Place Maubert because in a dark and hollow voice she would stubbornly shout at those around her: *I respect La Place Maubert; I don't give a damn about you!* No one knew of such a place, but it was assumed that for her it possessed a sacredness that no one dared challenge.

Sacredness was a word that was often used.

Occasionally, Jane would provoke the woman and, in the affected manner of a child, ask her where this "square" was located. Then the unhappy patient would grab hold of Jane, throw her long arms around the girl, and lift her high into the air with an astonishing and unexpected strength. As if the slender Jane were a sacrifice to be delivered to an invisible or vanished God, who for all eternity had turned His face away from every one of them; a sacrifice to be placed on an altar, just as Abraham had done, to appease the wrathful God.

But then a benefactor would come to her rescue. Never far away from this frightening and shocking scene would be Perdrix, a big, mannish woman who in conversation could demonstrate surprising aptitude and intellectual balance, but the movements of her body were not coordinated with her mind. Her body wandered around the square independently, so to speak, kicking and twitching, jumping with both feet over the sewer drains. Perdrix had made it a habit to observe Jane, or rather to keep watch over her, from a distance. And when the girl's life was threatened by the feared La Place Maubert, she would rush over to tear the screaming Jane out of the arms of the insane woman, kissing her tenderly and telling her to hide from the fearsome adversary. Incidentally, it was this wise and good Perdrix, with her peculiar twitches, whom the legendary actress Sarah Bernhardt sought out—on the advice of the art- and theater-minded Professor Charcot—as inspiration when studying for her role as *the authentic fool, who with her artistically developed twitches revealed the dark depths of her psyche.*

Their meeting was a complete failure, however. When Perdrix realized the purpose of the actress's visit, she simply turned around in anger, hitched up her skirt to show her naked backside, and with signals and gestures directed the astonished artiste to the hospital's main entrance, where she was promptly sent packing, accompanied by the roaring laughter of the inmates.

The actress later contacted Blanche Wittman. But that was after the rumors about Blanche had spread among the intellectual circles of Paris. This time she wanted to hear about quite different matters, about which the future torso in the wooden box was said to possess the secret.

6.

"The Fools' Dance," which Jane once asked about when she visited Blanche Wittman to *retrieve a memory*, must have been launched around the middle of Lent in 1884 during a masquerade ball in which the women patients took part along with a number of nurses and doctors.

Jane was dressed as "La descente de la Courtille." Her costume consisted of a man's shirt with the sleeves rolled up, a wide red belt around a pair of knickers, with loose trousers on top, and a little hat with a plume.

Her face was hidden behind a wolf's mask.

It's her first dance. She dances the polka with a man dressed as a medieval knight, and when he later removes his mask she discovers that he's one of the young doctors she likes very much.

None of Toulouse-Lautrec's paintings do her justice.

During those years she was a butterfly. The Book of Questions presents an evasive answer to the question of how she looked: *Jane was also a butterfly that had escaped from heaven.* The young doctor gave her a bouquet of lilies of the valley on the first of May.

Before the ball, Blanche helped her dress.

Blanche is one the women at Salpêtrière whom Jane admires because she's one of the stars. Blanche gives her a warm smile and tells her to have a good time.

She has a good time.

She starts dancing and discovers that she weighs nothing; she is flying and the music is carrying her. Freed from herself, she invents the new dance steps that later cause such a sensation at the Moulin Rouge. The crowd thins out around her; she keeps on dancing all alone in the middle. They applaud, they look at her; she is now sixteen years old and without burdens of any kind. What am I doing! she cries. She takes a break, goes over to Blanche and asks her something to do with her fear of creating a scandal.

Blanche leans forward and whispers.

Jane Avril then resumes dancing, even wilder. She discovers that she not only lacks any talents other than being able to dance, she is also lacking in memory, guilt, despair; she is freed from her mother, from her admirers, from rats, beatings, and slaps; she is cut off from the hospital, her memory is amputated, she feels very light, the new and impossible dance steps come easily to her, she is sixteen years old and she knows at this moment that she is absolutely free and there is nothing that can hold her back.

As soon as the music stops, she hesitates for a second but then keeps on dancing, in utter silence, while everyone watches her, as if she truly were a butterfly that has escaped from heaven.

A butterfly! That thrice repeated image with which the torso in the wooden box, in a certain sense, lived and died.

But what was it Blanche had whispered?

For a moment Jane looks at Blanche's face and realizes that this woman is in despair, and terrified, like an abandoned child. She has no idea why. That moment of freedom! and then a long life of chasing after that moment, like the addict's hunt for the memory of the first rush; the hunt, the dream of reclaiming that moment, the flight backwards, the hunt! the hunt! and she will never find her way back.

Then the applause. *That brief moment when anything is possible. That is the moment of love,* writes Jane. *How I regret that I can't seize that moment when anything is possible and remain forever in that instant.*

The conflict with Blanche, she writes, began at that moment. Charcot had witnessed her dance and applauded with a laugh.

"How lightly you move," he told her afterwards. "You ought to become a dancer. You have a rich life ahead of you. When I watch you I wish I were young again."

"And if you were?" she asked.

She was forced to leave Salpêtrière on July 11, 1884. Then she disappears from the story, or into it. What happens is that someone leaves, in a sense both leaving the story and starting it.

Jane Avril's last months at Salpêtrière are mysterious, but a few pieces of the puzzle can later be found in the Book of Questions.

She would return to Blanche and Marie on that memorable afternoon of April 12, 1913. Her life after that is almost a blank. Even Toulouse-Lautrec's drawings cease.

She was certainly not particularly ill at Salpêtrière, neither hysterical nor impaired; she could walk, she could dance. Nothing at the Castle, which is still there, contains any trace of her. Only the drawings from the following years say anything about Jane; but nothing about that first dance. The drawings made her world famous, even though she herself sank into oblivion. Perhaps that's what she wanted to ask about when she visited Blanche, who for her part can be seen in only one painting, the one with Professor Charcot in front of the spectators, when she's powerless.

The pictures of Jane say nothing about Salpêtrière.

Jane Avril was discharged. The only remnants of her mental illness, which may not have existed or may have been cured at Salpêtrière, are odd little quivers in her nostrils that make her nose twitch like a rabbit's.

III

THE SONG OF THE FLATBED WAGON

1.

I OFTEN IMAGINE THAT THE MEETING OF BLANCHE, JANE AVRIL, and Marie was quite pleasant, rather tranquil, and happy. The comments in the Book of Questions are brief. There is one offhand and surprising remark: *At least now I can keep food down.*

That was the first and last meeting between Marie and Jane Avril, a month before Blanche died. It was the only time the three women were together. Blanche made note of the meeting in the Book of Questions, on the last page.

She had undoubtedly thought of it as a starting point.

The other two women had rolled Blanche in her wooden box out to the terrace, and that's where they sat. Marie said something about the fact that at least she could keep food down. That's when they realized that she might survive.

They looked out at the trees; it was quite pleasant, and then they never saw each other again.

After Marie's breakdown when her lover Paul left her, and after the second Nobel Prize in 1911, the one for chemistry,

Blanche records only very brief remarks in the Book of Questions, and she never uses the word "love."

It's as if she has grown weary, or is seized with rage.

The second notebook, the black one, is different from the other two. Marie's breakdown is only touched on in strangely poetic images: they're in Paris, but the images are arctic.

Perhaps Blanche is writing about herself. If you're lying in a wooden box, it's natural to dream about expeditions to Greenland. Then she disguises herself as Marie, who moves through a snowy landscape, trudging through deep snow up toward a dark and abandoned house, buried in an icy grave, crushed beneath falling trees in a snowy landscape.

Blanche writes with her right hand. That's the one still remaining.

I haven't described the cart.

After the last amputation, Blanche moved about less and less, spending most of her time in bed. But to give her a certain mobility, Marie had a small, wagon-like cart constructed so that Blanche, sitting in the wooden box, and with the help of her hands (or hand!) could roll herself around the room.

And then suddenly a prose poem appears about Professor Marie Curie on an expedition across the arctic ice fields; cheerful! and in a wooden cart!

She wants to present images as some sort of solace. She claims to be writing down Marie's dreams. One of them is about the death of her beloved husband.

It's the one about the bird in the fog.

Blanche writes that Marie awoke at 3:45 on the morning after Pierre's death, and the dream seemed utterly real. She put her hand to her face and stroked her cheek, to confirm that she was awake: the dream had been very real, and she was very close to the answer. She was standing near a lake, on the shore. It was not the sea, not Saint-Malo, but an inland lake, maybe in Poland, a lake in the vicinity of Zakopane.

Out over the lake a strange morning fog was still hovering; the dark had lifted, but there was still a gray blanket drifting above, almost like a reflection of the darkness. It hung perhaps ten meters above the surface of the water, which was perfectly still and shiny, like quicksilver. That's where the birds were. They were sleeping, nestled in themselves and their dreams. She thought: Is that how birds dream? The fog was hovering so low that it left only the water and birds visible. No distant shores, only the wide expanse of motionless water. Perhaps an endless sea, although she wasn't sure.

Marie then pictured herself on an outermost shore, and in front of her nothing.

An outermost boundary. And then the birds, nestled in their dreams.

Suddenly a movement, a bird rising. She didn't hear a sound, merely saw the bird beat its wings against the surface of the water, free itself, and rise up at an angle: it happened suddenly but easily, the bird almost weightless. She saw it rise up, heading toward the gray ceiling of fog, and then vanish.

Not a sound did she hear.

She stood motionless on the shore, waiting for the dream to continue, for a solution to become visible, but nothing happened. Then she awoke and thought that maybe that was how Pierre had died. Like a bird that takes off and ascends and is suddenly gone.

Free, she thought, released. Then she thought: alone.

She stared at the ceiling. No beauty whatsoever, no freedom; she remembered that Pierre was dead and felt ordinary despair and grief pour in through the dawn. The dream dispersed. Suddenly she was unsure.

Maybe the dream wasn't about Pierre but about herself.

Later Marie tried to explain *the geographical background*.

The explanation was simple, Marie said. She was twelve years old. This was in Zakopane. She was about to sled down a hill; the slope was steep, the clouds hung low, spreading out like a blanket over the middle of the hill. She was a little frightened, in the breathless sort of way that she loved. They were calling her from the bottom of the slope; invisible voices from the foot of the cloud: Come on, Marie!

She knew that if she went she would feel terrified, and free.

So she took a deep breath. Marie! Marie! And she took off. That was the entire meaning of the dream. That's how she thought of love.

2.

Marie! Marie! And she took off.

Simple? No, not so simple.

Pierre was her third love, she confided to Blanche. The first two were in her youth, in Poland.

The third was Pierre.

She remembered the first time she saw Pierre Curie. He was standing at a balcony window, and he looked endearing. Later they had a discussion about a novel by Zola, and about the plausibility of the miracles at Lourdes. They began corresponding. They both admitted to having frostbite of the soul. That's why neither of them was able to love again.

She uses the expression "frost damage."

Three years later they were married, and eventually they had two children. Then Pierre died. That was the whole story, in brief outline. I'm forgetting one thing. They were jointly awarded the Nobel Prize in physics.

Now the story is complete. That was Marie's third love.

And the fourth?

She recalls how the fourth love began, the one with Paul Langevin, the one after Pierre's death.

It began on June 2, 1903.

She had defended her doctoral thesis on that day. She was happy. The opposition! the contempt for women at the university! the fact that she was one of only two women out of nine thousand at the Sorbonne to defend their doctorates! But she had fought her way through. She recalled the solemn mood that had reigned over the university hall. Her relatives from Poland had come. Everything had proceeded well.

And then the evening!

The newly married Ernest Rutherford, still young and not yet world famous, had arrived unannounced to pay a visit to the Curies' laboratory, but he was told that everyone was at the university hall for Marie's doctoral defense. So he went to see Paul Langevin, who lived with his family in a house opposite Montsouris Park. He made arrangements for a celebration and invited the Curies.

It's then, as Blanche writes, that Marie is struck by this Paul, like a billiard ball by a cue! and rolls like a billiard ball! though without comprehending.

After dinner the entire party went out to the gardens, led by Paul Langevin, who amiably offered Marie his arm.

Pierre Curie then took out a wand half-covered with zinc sulfide; *it contained a fair amount of radium solution that glowed brightly in the dark. It was, Marie thought, a magnificent finale to an unforgettable day. And everyone, especially Paul, was enchanted by the glow, which made her happy.*

*   *   *

She said the words *enchanted by the glow* with a kind of child-like joy, which, as it says in the Book of Questions, completely took Blanche's breath away.

Marie had many faces; one was the childlike face that she couldn't control. Later, terrified, she assumed a different face, *a different tone,* and became scientific; *the calm world-famous face* that Blanche sometimes called the *hysterical and catatonic one.* In a conversation with Blanche, Marie claimed that her third love, meaning Pierre Curie, was quite extraordinary, and they also had two children.

Yet her subsequent fourth love was deadly. She knew this; that was its allure. Blanche often asked Marie why she chose to destroy everything—her reputation, career, and happiness—for this utterly unnecessary fourth love. She knew, after all, that it had a touch of the banal about it and was not worthy of her; and a married man! *Yes! yes! yes! yes! yes!!!* Marie would then reply. *Enough!*

As if this desperate answer could explain the desperation!

At their first encounter, at the beginning of her fourth love—she actually does use this matter-of-fact sort of language; she was, after all, a respected mathematician—something inexplicable had glowed brightly in the dark. That was the image to which Marie would cling. At her encounter with her third love, Pierre, nothing like this existed.

Which meant: no allure of death. Nor was it like Blanche's love for Charcot, which is what the Book of Questions actually claims to be about.

That word "actually"!

At her first encounter with Pierre Curie, he discussed Émile Zola's novel *Lourdes* and called the miracles at Lourdes "a blasphemy against the scientific spirit." Marie agreed; she recounted this first conversation to Blanche.

"Everyone has a little poem in their past," Blanche then said, "something that, at a mature age, is later presented as a blasphemy against the scientific spirit!" And then, with a laugh, Blanche added that at Salpêtrière Hospital she had *experienced more miracles than the little saint at Lourdes could ever have dreamed.*

Marie merely stared at her with astonishment.

The marriage of Pierre and Marie would become legendary. Their happiness is one the best documented love stories.

In the face of what the future would designate as *historic love,* there is a great responsibility if you're one of those involved.

3.

But Blanche doesn't know what love "actually" is.

She writes about it, but only about what she doesn't understand. If you try to explain what you do understand, it's impossible.

Take, for example, the case of Pasqual and Maria Pinon!

Pasqual Pinon was a Mexican monster who worked in the mines; a monster with a double head. The other head was a woman's. Her name was Maria. In the 1920s they toured the west coast of America in a freak show. Her head grew out of his; he wore her like a miner wears his headlamp. She was beautiful. She was also jealous of him; if he talked to other women, she would sing horribly. She didn't actually make a sound, but he would practically explode with pain. In its way, theirs was a normal marriage.

Writing about them would show what normal love was. That was the idea.

It's impossible. *"They lived and died, each other's captive. At first unhappily, later—well, it was undoubtedly happiness. He wore her like a miner wears his headlamp; through this lamp fell darkness and light, it was nothing out of the ordinary.*

"*In the mirror he could see her face: her eyes opening and closing; the helplessly blinking eyelids, like those of a captured fawn; her lips trying to shape words that never reached him. She had no vocal cords, after all. He would often gently touch her cheek, out of helplessness. He would have liked to kiss her but he couldn't. When he looked at her in the mirror, he thought she was beautiful. He didn't want to hold her captive, but he did hold her captive. There was a period when she hated him for that.*

"*Later she understood.*

"*She was held captive in his head, he captive in hers. Held captive by each other, they lived close to the outermost boundary; their marriage was a state that was not out of the ordinary, though perhaps more clear. All his life he wore her, first with fury and hatred, later with patience and resignation, finally with love.*

"*During their last years he always slept with his hand against her cheek.*"

4.

Marie! Marie! And then she took off.

Another question, formulated much later in the Book of Questions, in a different tone of voice: **What did Marie mean at this time by love?**

It's necessary to fumble our way forward. Not give up.

Marie was happy when, upon receiving a monetary donation from Baron Edmond de Rothschild, she was able to acquire ten tons of pitchblende slag, which was what remained after extracting uranium and which everyone, aside from Marie and Pierre Curie, regarded as worthless.

Marie was happy when the sacks containing the brown slag, mixed with pine needles, arrived. She instructed Blanche on how to handle the material; it was strenuous labor. Marie and

Blanche had to process as much as twenty kilos of the raw material at a time, and everywhere in the carriage house, which they called the "laboratory," stood huge vessels brimming with various sediments and solutions.

"It was hard to move the containers, to pour the solutions and stand there stirring the seething mass in the cast-iron pot for hours at a time so as to separate out the radium from the barium, which was more difficult than isolating polonium from bismuth."

That's when Marie puts into words the dream she was having about love.

"Pierre and I were completely engrossed in penetrating the new field that had opened to us, thanks to the discovery of radium, which was so unexpected. And we were very happy even though the work conditions were so trying. We spent all our days in the laboratory, most often eating a meager, simple student's lunch on-site. A great calm reigned over our shabby, tumbledown carriage house. Now and then, as we kept watch over some process, we would take a stroll out in the yard and talk about our work, both what we were in the midst of and what we were planning. When we got cold, we would warm up with a cup of tea, which we drank in front of the stove.

"We lived as if in a dream, completely engrossed in our thoughts."

Love for her work, but also for Pierre.

Blanche writes it all down, her tone hopeful, almost enthusiastic. As if in a painting depicting a lacemaker, head bowed, serious, grave, her body not visible; that's how we have to picture Blanche as she sits in her box, with both legs amputated, increasingly obsessed with finding the key to love, passion, and life. Blanche Wittman, a sensual legend of the nineteenth century, the object of so much secret adoration by all those men who observed her but were not allowed to touch!

And how she would understand, sitting there in her box.

Blanche tries tirelessly to understand.

The scientific work to trace and isolate the substance that as yet had no name but would later be called radium was a *grueling and exciting undertaking*, Blanche writes. She strongly identifies with Marie, almost arrogantly so; a laboratory assistant who was once world famous as *something else*: a medium at Salpêtrière Hospital. What presumptuousness.

What could she teach Marie?

Pierre is hardly mentioned in the Book of Questions; he has been jealously erased. *Marie and I would stand there all day long, stirring the seething mass with a heavy iron bar that was almost as tall as we were. We were often aching with fatigue by the end of the day. Yet Marie was happy because her attempts to isolate radium during those years were meeting with success. But oh, what great difficulties she encountered; she had to work with such care and precision with fractionated crystallization in her attempts to concentrate radium. She would often grow annoyed at the ever-present iron filings and soot, from which she had a hard time protecting her precious products. But the despondency that occasionally descended on her after some effort that brought only meager results never lasted long, giving way instead to a renewed interest in her work. That's why she was able to report, finally, in July 1902, that she had succeeded in isolating one decigram of radium. She gave its atomic weight as 225, thus placing it after barium in Mendeleyev's periodic table, in the column with alkaline earth metals.*

Those were the first years of the twentieth century. At the same time she presents, without arrogance, an account of *the genesis of the modern world*. Sometimes Pierre Curie is present, sometimes Blanche; someone asks questions, someone writes; sometimes Blanche, sometimes Marie. And always at the center is a substance called radium, mysteriously radiant, flickering like love, not yet deadly.

If you're seeking a new world, you can't be afraid of the old mud that is clinging to your legs.

During the last year of Pierre's life, the Curies developed a great interest in a woman medium by the name of Eusapia Palladino, who traveled the globe to "establish contacts between the worlds of the living and the dead." She was born in an Italian mountain village. As a child she had fallen and knocked a hole in her head. According to one theory, it was out of this hole that a "cold vapor" would come whenever she was in a trance.

She could also make chairs dance.

Pierre and Marie Curie met her for the first time in 1905. They studied her at a number of seances and could find no explanation. And why should they, when the radiation of radium could not yet be explained? Yet on the afternoon of the day he died, Pierre spoke at the Physics Society about the phenomenon of Eusapia Palladino and made an enthusiastic appeal for the "convincing and real nature of the phenomenon."

Two hours later he was dead. That was that. And why not? What distinguishes Blanche's search from Pierre's, or from Marie's?

5.

Marie's first two loves were in Poland.

That was before Marie left for loves number three and four, before her time in Paris. Yet perhaps her very first love was her native land of Poland. She was often enraged, but was it against the Czarist tyranny or something else? As a thirteen-year-old, during a discussion of Shakespeare's *Othello*, she lashed out in a

furious attack on Desdemona: *No! I say no! What kind of charac-*
ter is "sweet Desdemona," who would allow a slap in the face without
a word of protest! Only a fool would allow such a thing! One of
Marie's friends assured her that a loving wife would allow more
than that if it were necessary to placate her husband, but Marie
then furiously replied that *a person who is affronted in the most seri-*
ous manner would choose death! and then continued in a very different direction: *I can tolerate an insult, and even forgive it, if it's aimed*
solely at myself and no one else, but I would never forgive an affront to
my native land!

She left her first two loves behind, as if shedding a snake
skin, Blanche writes with surprising venom. It was the same
with love as with the Polish culture and the Polish language.
Tyranny forced love below the surface. Until finally love broke
free. In this sense it was a liberating movement and thus deadly,
although emancipated. The Russian oppressors persecuted the
principles of love in every aspect, and for that reason instruction
in the Polish language and Polish culture had to continue in
secret, for the sake of love.

Of the first man, a young officer, we have only a name and
a portrait. He couldn't control her and was left behind.

She also left her second love behind, and *rejoiced at what had*
been on her way to Paris and her research.

Pictures show her tightly corseted with a very small waist
and protruding bosom. All her life she was regarded as beautiful,
and sensual, with the exception of her hands, which early on
became damaged from burns and deformed by radiation from
the radium. *In the ecstasy of love she would hide her hands in the*
other's hair, as if from love but perhaps from shame, Blanche remarks
in the Book of Questions. Her hands were scarred. Love had
burned itself into her hands, as if she were an animal and radium a branding iron.

Blanche often makes use of imagery. The one about the
branding iron and radium occurs repeatedly.

The enigmatic blue color, which might be radiation. And they keep trying to explain it.

Marie's reaction to Pierre's death?

In the dossier about the double-headed Mexican monster Pasqual Pinon and his wife Maria, there is something in the death scene.

Perhaps there. Oh, if only it were to be found there!

"He died on the evening of April 21, 1933, in a hospital in Orange County near Los Angeles. The nurse who took care of him during his last year, and whose name was Helen, remained sitting at his side the whole time. His death was without pain. When he died and the big, dark face grew still and his arm sank, then it was like a bird that lifts off from the lake, soundless and light, climbs through the night fog, and is gone: utterly silent, serene. And then it's gone.

"According to the journalists, Maria died eight minutes after he did.

"When he died, she at first opened her eyes wide, with a look of inexpressible terror, as if she instantly understood what had happened; her lips, which all her life had tried to articulate some message, moved as if she were appealing for help. But once again not a sound came from them. No sounds. For several minutes it seemed as if she were desperately trying to shout a message to someone out there, maybe it was to him; maybe, terrified, she was trying to call him back. But the bird had taken off, the night fog again hung motionless above the lake, and she was alone.

"What was it she wanted to shout? No one knows. You shouldn't try to explain love. But what would we be if we didn't try?

"Then she suddenly grew perfectly calm, and her eyes filled with tears. The bird had taken off, and she was alone; that was the second time they saw her cry. The first time was when she was sitting on the steps of the house trailer, when the crisis had passed, and the Dog Man stroked her cheek with the wing feathers of a bird. This was now the second time, but she was calm. She was ready to take the unprecedented step into a

brief solitude, move right out into the dizzying void, but she could do it. She lay still now, staring straight up, staring right through everything as if nothing could stop her. Then her lips slowly parted, forming a very faint but discernible smile. She closed her eyes, and died. That was eight minutes after he died.

"*For eight minutes she was alone.*"

Pierre and Marie both regarded themselves as individuals on the periphery of life. There, on the outskirts, they were conjoined in a search for the secret. It is this symbiosis that is the secret of love, Marie explained to Blanche.

Conjoined?

Marie was an outsider; she had grown up with Mickiewicz poems and the Polish patriots' furious and inflammatory appeals! the fire! the call! the language! That's how she loved to describe the way it was.

Then she met Pierre, who was the grandson of a Communard.

It's possible to picture him as one of the officers that Marie deserted in her youth: it's possible to picture him as enormously strong, as a defender, even as a Communard; but suddenly she saw how ill he was, and fragile.

That coughing. His face pale as death.

Why did these impassioned lovers of radium turn so strangely pale?

Yes, they became completely washed out, diluted.

Was it the flickering blue light? Perhaps it was the symbolic blue light, or the blue of decadence, or Huysman's blue perfumer's organs: everyone could interpret the blue light of the new century in his own way. It was as if people sensed that the ensuing century would be mysterious and shocking, and the metaphors were colored by this! Perfumer's organs! Medusa!

But was love deadly too? the illnesses inexplicable? life washed out? What was wrong with Pierre? What did the doctors know?

The doctors and science knew nothing. They couldn't even say what was wrong with the extraordinary woman Blanche Wittman, Blanche! the medium! the hysteric from Salpêtrière who became healthy and strong along with several thousand other hysterical women, but only after Charcot died! the woman who now sat there in her wooden box and wrote.

Did she and Marie write the great poem of the new century?

Pierre couldn't sleep at night because of the pain in his back.

He thought his spine was decaying. They traveled to Carolles, then to Saint-Malo; it was the same coast where Charcot had once, many years earlier, put a hollow reed in his brother's mouth as the tide waters slowly rose. Blanche had told this story to Marie, who was surprised, incredulous. *He covers up the crime of love with another offense!* But Pierre was now walking, hunched and silent, along the shore that was swept clean of any tide waters. Was it leukemia? or cancer? Why was he so silent?

He was forty-six years old. He was always tired. They sometimes quarreled about this. On the last day Marie stayed behind in Saint-Rémy to lie in the sun. Pierre took the train to the city. They had quarreled. She didn't want to be left alone.

Not even for eight minutes! Not even for that long!

And yet her dream about the bird that rises up and is free. The icy plateau. And much later: the dream of love on the way to death in Nome.

As a young man, Pierre told Marie, he had been through a love experience that was painful. The young woman he loved had died, only twenty years of age.

This was all he recounted. "Died" was the word that he used. Not "committed suicide" or "took her own life after I betrayed her" or "quietly passed away believing in her Savior."

She died. He felt guilty.

He then promised himself to live the rest of his life as a celibate. Then he met Marie, he told her the story, they married, they had two children, and he died.

Frost damage of the soul! A thorn in the side of love!

Marie always believed that the story about the young woman who died was fiction. That he, quite simply, was terrified by Marie. That she was much too alive for him. She complained to Blanche: Why are all men so terrified of women who are thoroughly alive that they mistake strength for death, and flee?

"It's true," Blanche replied. "You're not strong, but you're alive, and that's terribly frightening for those who don't understand."

That's what she said. Blanche! That woman! In her wooden box! Severed! Shortened to a torso! Constantly holding this notebook! And believing that she is basically talking about herself!

It's disgusting.

I'm writing this during the autumn, the trees are stripped of leaves. Soon the snow will arrive; what a relief. I keep returning to Pasqual Pinon and his Maria. Is it possible ever to be done with them? And then the dread that if I am done with them, then an answer will be found that obliterates everything.

An answer must not be found.

Blanche in her rolling wooden box, and with her obsession for Marie's loves. Why did she cling so tightly to Marie Curie? *Marie! Marie! And then it started.*

It's not an easy thing to be rid of Marie and surrender to Blanche, as she sits there in her makeshift box.

* * *

Marie imagined that the concepts of love and guilt were inextricably united.

That's why Pierre's solitary wandering on the last evening of his life was so crystal clear for her. He was to make his last guilt-filled wandering toward death in the increasingly heavy downpour, and it was her fault because it wasn't him that she loved but rather their shared expedition into the dark continent, which was the twentieth century. But that's not something that could be said. That's nothing but cynicism.

Perhaps she wanted to be free.

That's why she was constantly assuring Pierre that she was completely bound to him. Which was also true. Reassuring him of her love became her life's goal. Then they quarreled on that last day; it was one of their more intense and exhausting quarrels, neither long nor brief, just exhausting. Afterwards he took the train to Paris, and she never saw him again.

6.

The story of Marie's third love ended around 6 p.m. on April 19, 1906, when Pierre lost his life at the place where rue Dauphine converges with Pont-Neuf.

It was raining. There was heavy traffic at the intersection. Pierre had stepped into the roadway to cross the street when, according to the police report, a nine-meter-long wagon "fully loaded with fabric for uniforms" and pulled by two very big old nags, swung onto the road at great speed from Pont-Neuf. The driver, a retired milk truck driver by the name of Louis Manin, then caught sight of a tram coming from the right along Quai Conti and reined in his horses, but the tram driver signaled for the wagon driver to proceed. Manin had almost crossed the intersection when a figure appeared from behind a passing cab. It was the famous Nobel Prize winner in physics Pierre Curie, who was struck by the shoulder of one of the horses and tried to take hold of the animal's mane. Then both horses reared up, and the man, who was only later identified as the Nobel Prize winner Curie, seemed to have trouble moving agilely. In reality, he had appeared strangely powerless and weak-willed, perhaps because of some illness of which the driver Manin naturally had no knowledge, nor did anyone else at that moment or even later.

In short: the man fell in the street.

The driver then tried to steer his team to the left, and the front wheel of the heavily loaded wagon, which was transporting large bundles of uniform fabric, actually managed to avoid the prostrate Nobel Prize winner, but the rear wheel, which was reinforced with iron, rolled right over Curie's head, crushing it. The wagon weighed six tons.

Death was instantaneous and occurred, as the newspapers would recount, at the same moment that reports arrived about the great earthquake in San Francisco. And during this same time period a great religious revival was taking place in Los Angeles, where a black preacher by the name of William Seymour underwent a Spirit baptism and was touched by tongues of fire, just like during the first Whitsuntide, as described in the Acts of the Apostles. And then the gift of a thousand tongues descended from heaven and he spoke in tongues and a great revival was started which would later be called the Pentecostal movement, and which, like the spark that ignited a prairie fire, caused everything to burn! the prairie! passion! love! And in this way, in the rain, with blood, with confusion, with reason, and in an attempt to step into the dark future of humanity, the twentieth century began. Like that! Precisely like that! With a series of events that did not seem to have any connection, and Marie was told: he's dead, he's dead, yes, he is. Is there no one who will take pity on the woman! You can see what a state she's in!

They summoned his wife Marie, and she came. And he was dead. Nothing to be done about it. We all have to die. Though he was very young.

And then didn't she have to take the dizzying step into solitude?

That was how Marie's third love ended. His head was crushed. Not at all like a bird that rises from the surface of the water and disappears into the fog; no, his skull was quite simply crushed by the six-ton wagon, and that was that.

And so it was over. This is what made Marie realize why she loved him so terribly, and this is what Blanche recorded in her book, in order to understand, and she never gave up.

Marie, Maria. And so it led straight into the dizzingly black hole, which was the deepest darkness of the sea.

7.

They went to see her and told her that he was dead.

Blanche asked: How did he look? Marie didn't understand; she was sitting on the floor next to the wooden cart, having locked the door to keep out the others. How did he look? You have to tell me how he looked, Marie, or I'll go mad. I won't, Marie said. You will, Blanche replied. You saw him. You have to tell me, as if it were a funeral picture you're holding in front of you; how did he look? His face, said Marie, was peaceful. His lips, which I used to say belonged to a *gourmand*, were pale and colorless. Then she fell silent. Go on, said Blanche. There must have been an enormous amount of bleeding, said Marie, I can't tell you anything else. Go on, said Blanche. What a horrific impact, whispered Marie, you could hardly see his hair under the clotted blood, *because that's where the wound is*, and on the right side you could see the frontal bone sticking out.

Then she didn't say another word all afternoon. As if with these words she had recounted the entire secret of her love for Pierre. And made Blanche realize how dreadful it was to discover love just as it dashed off forever, in the rain, across the street, beneath the horses, beneath the ironclad wheel, swiftly and not beautifully, not like the bird that rises up, but gone.

For three years she kept silent. And everyone knew that Madame Curie had now entered into the gray mental illness that is called grief, and she did so because only now did she realize what she loved and that it was too late.

And the only only only one she could tell this to was Blanche, the little amputated monster in the wooden cart, the woman who had once experienced love and learned love's painful lesson and innermost secret.

Marie! Go on! Don't stop! Don't look back!

I've always wondered what it's like for the one who survives when a love comes to an end almost before it has begun. If you wonder you have to find out, and reconstruct it. Nothing wrong with that.

My own father died when I was six months old. Amputated from me, the innocent child! Without grief or regrets! At least that's what people said. It happened in March. Afterwards Mamma caught the bus from the small clinic in Bureå, and the bus let her off down by the wood-chip mill and she trudged through the snow up to the edge of the forest where our house stood. It was late at night and the house was dark; a neighbor who lived near Hedmans was taking care of me while he died. A month earlier someone in town had predicted that three men would die, and three men died. He had dreamed that three pine trees fell, then awoke and understood. It was an omen. Everything surrounding death was filled with secret signs that could be interpreted, like poetry. Death evoked poetry from the forest workers, but these Norrland woodcutters could hardly avoid dreaming every night about trees that fell: trees were always falling, after all. A pine tree had fallen on a neighbor, who lay pinned in the deep snow for twenty hours; there he was found, frozen to death. His right arm had been free, and he used his finger to draw his last words in the snow: YOU DARLING MARIA I, and then he couldn't stretch out his arm any farther. Poetry? More like an obituary. Trees were always falling, but not all trees signified something; you learned to distinguish between one sort of dream and another.

The bus driver, it was Marklin, had stopped at the woodchip mill and turned around to ask the others in the bus whether there was someone who would take pity on her; that's how he expressed it: *take pity on her*. But she didn't want any help because she was feeling so miserable and didn't want to show it.

He was young when he died, after all. It's a relief to stop thinking about Blanche and Marie and Pierre to think about him instead. Amputated! I traveled north to visit the last of his brothers. He still wept easily at the mention of my father. We all do in my family. And everyone who knew my father had *recollections* but no one could really tell me what he was like. I still have the funeral pictures, the photographs of him in his coffin. Hoppla! Hoppla!! There was a plethora of funeral pictures from that time, and in some of them he looks so much like me that the world toppled and practically disappeared, but I steeled myself. No one could tell me what he was like. *We had plenty of recollections but no more than that.* Almost seventy years had passed, after all; what was there to remember? And no doubt it was the same for Marie Skłodowska Curie. It was easier to describe the frontal bone sticking out, but what he was like disappeared in the telling.

"Marie," said Blanche, "then tell me what he was like, not how he looked." But Marie couldn't do it, and so she entered into the long period of waiting, which was the void before her fourth love appeared. The void and despair lasted for three years, followed by something else. But for the woman who got out of

Marklin's bus and trudged through the deep snow up to the house, it lasted her whole life, and nothing came afterwards. You might ask yourself about the justice of this, but perhaps Blanche had an answer in her notebooks, the ones that possessed the secret of love, the love that existed or was acquired or the love that was always denied someone.

Marie, Maria. And then it started.

What was it about Marie that reminded me of my mother?

Someone is walking up toward the house in the forest, through deep snow, thirty-two years old, beautiful, quiet, despairing and not yet as hard as the fathomless absence of love can make a person. And ahead lie fifty-six years of lone-liness, which she chose voluntarily, in her foolishness. But Marie took the step straight into the black, dizzying darkness of love; it was quite marvelous for six months, and then came the catastrophe.

But they both must have had an idea of what love ought to be. Wasn't that true? Damn it all, it must have been true.

For three long years Marie remained in Limbo.

Then she emerged. It was very surprising to everyone. Even her children had become accustomed to her living in grief, hav-ing decided never to abandon her grief. With a gray and expres-sionless face she took care of the little ones, then wrapped her-self up in Blanche and her work.

Then one day in April, without an invitation, she went to visit her old friends, the Borel family. She had coffee with them. She was not wearing her customary black dress but a white dress with a rose at the waist.

They could see that she was happy. Something had happened. She told them nothing. That was the beginning of the catastrophe.

Alone. But only for eight minutes!

It's not necessary to give in, after all. There is always something that is better than death. Who could blame her?

Plenty of people, as it turned out.

IV

THE SONG OF THE WAGON-MAKER'S SON

1.

THE STATUE OF CHARCOT OUTSIDE THE ENTRANCE TO SAL-pêtrière Hospital was melted down in 1942 by the Germans; the metal was transferred to the weapons industry. The portraits of him show his imperturbable stone-face; they were painted by contemporaries and display the image he wished to convey to the future.

Blanche must have seen right through him.

An abundance of texts about Charcot exist. Documents are always written by those who are able to write, as well as by the victors. It is also desirable that they be preserved, otherwise there is only silence. Yet this limits the scope of the truth. About the personal relationship between Charcot and Blanche there is almost nothing. Her own three-part Book of Questions is therefore unique.

No doubt she simply wanted to tell her own story, but she ended up slipping into Marie's. Perhaps she didn't fully realize that she herself was dying. Marie was something different, something grander. Tragedies ought to be grand, not like Blanche's peculiar amputated tragedy. As she sat there in her wooden box, perhaps it wasn't so easy to see that she was dying. That may be what happens.

A great deal of talk about love. Few answers.

But she does have a story.

2.

On the evening when he persuaded Blanche to accompany him on his last journey to Morvan, Charcot had a long and very personal conversation with her.

Surprisingly, he told her a great deal about the first part of his life, especially the years of his childhood.

The text is now calm in tone. It's evident that she loved him, in spite of everything that happened, and that she never harbored any hatred or mistrust toward him. He was *soft-spoken and endearing,* she writes, almost like on the last night at Morvan.

He was afraid of dying. When he talked about Saint-Malo, he seemed very young, and shy.

He was born in Paris, and spent one summer in Saint-Malo. That summer is the only one from his childhood that he mentions.

He says that he is afraid of the coast outside Saint-Malo. The coast was his great teacher. It was the tidal waters that frightened him; the difference between high and low tide was sixteen meters, and it was beyond his control. Whatever was beyond control was the most enticing and the most frightening; that was why he later devoted himself to this. That coast, he said, is like the human soul: the human being is laid bare and covered up according to rhythms determined by God's spirit. It's merely an image; it means nothing more: he is not a believer. *What is sacred in a human being is like the ebb and flow—it lays bare and covers up the human soul*—he says that he has respect for the labored breathing of the sea.

Everything that is so utterly uncovered is necessary and frightening. *To drain a person's interior so that crabs, marine plants, and mollusks become accessible, that frightened him.* In Saint-Malo on the French coast, on the English Channel, there was a vast low tide that exposed the shore for many kilometers. He and his younger brother would walk across the drained sea bottom and then, as the water slowly returned, they would follow the shifting shoreline in toward safety. First at a walk, playfully and feeling superior, then in a panic, with the tidal waters rolling over their feet and coming up to their knees and finally almost to their hips, until at last *the redemptive shore was reached by the two exhausted children.*

Charcot was afraid to feel the helplessness of facing death. When the time came, it was important to have finished everything important.

This was especially true of love. Then death would be like being flung into the terrible dark hole of eternity. When it came, he wanted to hold death itself by the hand, and say with a little smile, *it's already finished, come on.* What filled him with terror was what had not been finished. His love for Blanche was unfinished. He talked all night about the coast of Saint-Malo. He dwelled in particular on an incident when his brother was playing, recklessly, near a cliff by the shore, and during the game his foot got stuck between two rocks. At first his friends ignored his calls for help and didn't take his situation seriously, but when the water began to rise the boy's cries of distress grew shriller, and they saw the trouble he was in.

Charcot—who was the older brother—tried to pull his brother's foot free; the water was rising with unexpected speed but his foot was trapped and refused to budge. Someone ran for help. By then the water had reached the boy's chest, and they could see that he would drown in another fifteen or twenty minutes. Charcot recalls that his distressed brother's eyes were so filled with despair that Charcot, in his need, first turned to the

Savior Jesus Christ with a fervent prayer for mercy and forbearance. But his brother's desperate screams for help, *sounding like a
shrieking seagull*, became so heartrending that he cut short his
invocation and dashed up the beach to a heap of reeds that had
washed up on shore. He grabbed a bunch of these hollow reeds,
chose the longest one, and ran back to his brother, who only
with great effort was able to keep his head above water. He stuck
the reed into his brother's mouth and told him to breathe
through it if the water rose over his head. The water then
reached his brother's head and no rescue was yet in sight; pre-
sumably his foot could be freed by using a crowbar, for instance,
if some adult benefactor would come running with this crowbar in hand and amidst reassuring shouts would dash down to
the boy in distress. Charcot watched as his brother's desperate
and wildly staring eyes became submerged in the water; then a
hissing, panting sound could be heard from the top end of the
reed, the sound which proclaimed that the reed was allowing
life-giving air to be sucked down to his brother, who still had
his foot stuck in a lethal grip. Charcot held the reed upright
with his right hand, while with the other he desperately clutched
his brother's hand, and in that manner anxiously awaited the
sound of a benefactor's running footsteps, *a benefactor, perhaps
with a crowbar in hand* or, as it may have or should have turned
out, *with an ax or maybe a saw.*

   As she writes this in her Book of Questions, the tone is different once again, and more scientific. Here she is taking great
care to describe her lover's childhood and early career.
   He is the fourth son, and his mother dies when he is five.
They move back to Paris. His father was a wagon-maker, *but as
a child Charcot met many celebrities*—Blanche has underlined this
phrase as if it had special meaning. She mentions the painter
Delacroix but also the fact that Charcot was allowed to watch a

rehearsal of *Orpheus*. He was enchanted by it. In the neighbor-hood where he grew up there were many theaters and places of entertainment; he was often enchanted.

Enchantment is the recurring theme. She never mentions Charcot by his first name.

When he begins work at Salpêtrière Hospital he notes that the patients are living in filth and are *sexually undernourished*; they satisfy themselves in an almost manic fashion, and the approxi-mately six thousand women are *an unruly lot*—those are his exact words—but some of the patients display an *extraordinary theatrical talent*, and this artistic element both astonishes and enchants him. He mentions, without being prompted, Jane Avril. Blanche then inserts: *the one who danced like a butterfly that had escaped from heaven*. She remarks that he shows no reaction.

Perhaps he is also enchanted by this, but steels himself.

All the photographs of Charcot show a stony face, even though she writes time and again that he is "enchanted." His father's wagon customers were socially quite distinguished. During the rehearsal of *Orpheus*, Charcot noticed a singer who sang in a most enchanting manner. The masturbating women at Salpêtrière frightened him, but he was constantly steeling him-self. It was important to give them better food and to clean up the exceedingly filthy rooms.

He calls himself an enlightened man. He supports this notion by citing his social involvement in the patients' hygiene, and with his sense of enchantment.

His mother died in childbirth. The words "enchanted" and "steeling himself" keep recurring in the Book of Questions. When he rescued his brother he steeled himself and used the saw, and afterwards his brother thanked him profusely.

Charcot trained to be a doctor. His brother became a respected wagon-maker (one-legged), a soldier, and a seaman. Charcot was first in his graduating class. He *had a mind for the logic of Descartes' chain of reasoning*. He was once invited to visit the family home of a friend, and there he saw an animal skeleton which also sparked his interest in the human body and all its parts. He describes himself as a positivist and says that he studied the gaunt beggars on the sidewalks of Paris so he could better see and understand what makes up the interior of a human being: by this he still means nothing more than *the skeleton and parts of the body*. He is, he repeats, an enlightened man. He rejects religion as a stage in human development that ought to be overcome. He desires facts and details about what is incomprehensible. As a young doctor he arrives at Salpêtrière Hospital, and there he sees six thousand women locked up and living in hell; he does not use the word "hell" but describes the horrifying conditions in which they're living with empathy and intense curiosity.

Surely the words "intense curiosity" must be Blanche's own interpretation. She knew him, after all. *Ultimately*, she writes at the end of the Book of Questions, *the animals and I were the only ones he truly loved*. He did not believe in any God. When he once called to God and received no reply, he appropriated a saw. God's spirit was like the ebb and flow of the tide, uncovering and killing; the task of the human being was to rebel.

Did he really mean the saw?

In 1844 he moves to his own room in a small pension on rue Hautefeuille. He gets up at four-thirty every morning, washes in cold water, heats coffee over *the forbidden kerosene lamp* and then leaves to start his rounds at the hospital. He is still young. In pictures he looks endearing. He works at the hospital until lunchtime, and says that he then studies in the library between four and six before the lectures begin. Dinner is at seven-thirty. Then he studies until midnight. Charcot is still young and meticulous about hygiene since he can't see any other option or alternative.

At the hospital he doesn't want to become infected, like his mother, *who died in the loving hands of a pathologist*. That was in childbirth.

It's not innocence, or irony, but hatred that can be sensed in the word "loving." He washes often. During autopsies the bodies were not kept cold; they were merely soaked in formalin. Occasionally, as he walked home through the streets from the hospital, he would imagine that he smelled, and that people were looking at him with revulsion because of this. He is a completely normal young doctor, and he looks endearing. The first place he practices medicine is at a women's castle called Salpêtrière. What is he supposed to do?

He washes because the risk of infection is significant. He is an enlightened man. He has not yet begun to love animals more than people.

According to the Book of Questions, he tells Blanche: *We cannot avoid the filth of life.* He seems to have regarded the human being as a machine. He is still young; he is so young that it must be considered wrong to kill him, she writes very surprisingly. *When I picture this young scientist, the way he must have looked to those who saw him, my heart fills with love and the wish that I might have met him back then.* On the next page she adds, as an afterthought, that it is always wrong to kill someone, *because it goes against the principle of the sacredness of life.*

At the age of thirty-nine he marries Augustine Durvis, a widow with a seven-year-old daughter. By then he has his own practice with many prominent clients. When war breaks out in 1870, his family moves to London, but Charcot remains at the hospital, which for several months becomes a hospital for the wounded. He sympathizes with the Communards.

It's necessary to repeat that he is an enlightened man.

Hysteria fascinated Charcot because it presented *a mixture of chaos and order,* which appealed to him as an enlightened man. Within hysteria, he claimed, there was a certain system, a secret code, which, if revealed, could point the way to the meaning of life. This blend of chaos and order possessed an almost musical form; it was a composition in the form of andante, allegro, and adagio. The hysterical crises which he succeeded in evoking through the innovation of—or, as he also said, the discovery of—pressure points on the human body, these crises began with an aura, continued with epileptic, clonic convulsions, followed by the *attitudes passionnelles* which so astonished the spectators, and finally by the more relaxed and emotional phase.

It was the human being as a symphony. He had always wanted to be a composer.

Charcot addressed his patients in the informal manner, regardless of whether they came from the upper or lower class. Of composers, he was most delighted by Beethoven, Gluck, Mozart, and Vivaldi. He was good at drawing, especially skilled as a caricaturist, and he possessed a particular fascination with dwarves. Later on he became an animal-lover and owned a guenon, a type of monkey, by the name of Zibidie. There was a fundamental melancholia to his temperament that Blanche claims not to understand, and it makes her despair. Zibidie would be waiting for him every evening when he came home. He noted with delight that she seemed to have a built-in clock, *just as I do.* The monkey was always seated at the table in a high-chair next to Charcot and fed with a silver spoon. He was a good father, but he loved his guenon. She had her own napkin with an embroidered monogram. Whenever she menstruated she would be dressed in a pair of waxlike pink panties. Charcot claimed to have learned a great deal from the monkey, meaning things about human nature.

The monkey also had her *nervous days.*

At the height of his career and before the catastrophic love affair with Blanche which obliterated his scientific reason, he felt that animals were ultimately better than human beings. The word "disillusioned" recurs. He had children. Not a word about his relationship with his wife. He once said to Blanche: I often wish that I were the patient and not the doctor. Why? she asked him. He then stared at her, not with the usual endearing expression on his face, but with fury and despair; yet he hastily steeled himself and brushed aside her question with a joke.

On the house he bought in Neuilly he had chiseled into the facade a quote from Dante, in French.

It's from *The Inferno*, Canto 3, verse 49, and the quote, in its entirety, is as follows:

> Fame of them the world hath none,
> Nor suffers; Mercy and Justice scorn them both.
> Speak not of them, but look, and pass them by.

Such an extraordinary motto.

The third canto in *The Inferno* is about those who are indecisive and half-hearted, the gray multitudes who fall short because of doubt, or fear.

Is this a fragment of Charcot's self-image? Or of his arrogance before those who didn't dare break new paths?

Observe those who failed for lack of daring. And then leave them behind. That's what he had chiseled into the entrance of his home. That was before he met Blanche.

3.

The experiments that Charcot—and later Blanche—are trying to carry out can almost be likened to a religious rite. What did they involve?

A type of sorcery, intended to explain a measure of coherence?

Meaning those desperate passages about the "innermost nature" of love. Descriptions of the first experiments at the hospital, *introitus ad altar Dei,* but what does this have to do with love, or a person's desires? Power, perhaps?

No, not even power.

*   *   *

It is not known why he opened the experiments to the general public.

There's nothing wrong with taking the step from science into mysticism. He probably thought that's where the solution might be found, but he needed support. During the first lectures—all of which were later translated by Sigmund to German, unfortunately with some critical remarks for which Charcot never forgave his disciple—he relies closely on Paracelsus, and on Mesmer, in particular: as if he were tentatively trying to write himself into an occult tradition, but with apparent, rather unbecoming, skepticism.

He writes "with astonishment" about Mesmer's Paris sojourn and the way in which he, in 1778, with his vials of magnetic water achieved enormous popularity. And how, using his cane, he would energize his patients to health, and how he, so as not to lose his popularity among the poor, had a tree magnetized in the poor neighborhoods so they could heal themselves.

Otherwise no critical remarks.

Charcot says that the first experiments with women are experiments with hypnotism. It was a harmless word. That's the reason he uses it. He selects two younger women as subjects: Augustine (her last name has been lost, and after this experiment she disappears from the story) and Blanche Wittman.

His assistants are Gilles de la Tourette, Joseph Babinski, and Désiré-Magloire Bourneville, two of whom would later become monumental figures in medical history. He characterizes the initial state of the subjects, meaning the clients, as unstable. Augustine had been in a trancelike state since the previous day, and Blanche was aggressive, refractory, uttering brief bursts of laughter and regarding Charcot with almost hostile eyes. Nevertheless, the experiment began with Blanche, who was told to look at a pendulum; it took only five to eight minutes before she seemed to grow drowsy. She closed her eyes, and fell asleep.

She remained in a seated position.

Augustine was placed on a bed. When Charcot raised her eyelids for several seconds, she reacted at once by stretching out her legs, a movement that made her nightgown slip to the side and reveal her naked pelvis with her sex exposed. Charcot then gave Bourneville orders to cover her body.

Blanche was now asleep. Charcot blew gently at her face, telling her that when she awoke she would have a sense of well-being. Yet she remained in a cataleptic state. Charcot then used his hand to press on points near her ovaries: this is before Charcot invented the ovary press, the one made of metal and leather, which was used to stop hysteria. She awoke and looked at Charcot with a strange smile.

"How do you feel now?" asked Charcot.

She replied:

"I wouldn't say no to a brioche."

That was a type of bread. The four doctors regarded her with bewilderment.

"A brioche," she repeated, fixing an unwavering gaze on Charcot, who then looked away, as if in shame or fear. In a low voice he told his assistant Babinski—who would later become world famous as the one who defined certain nerve reflexes associated with the diagnosis of, for instance, syphilis: *Babinski's reflex*—he ordered this Babinski to bring her a brioche.

"What purpose will that serve?" asked Babinski.

Charcot did not reply. The brioche was brought. Babinski repeated his question, now in a louder voice, as if in anger.

That was the first experiment.

Charcot's assistants were astonished and shocked by the peculiar submissiveness he suddenly displayed with regard to Blanche. She had calmly devoured the brioche, watching Charcot intently, as if the others in the room did not exist.

The experiment was recorded in precisely this way. But warning bells should have sounded!

4.

In the end he came to think of death as a void in which Blanche did not exist. And he alone was to blame.

On his last night, in August 1893, he was frightened. If you suddenly believe that what you've done was built on shifting sand, then the darkness becomes terrifying. If, in this darkness, Blanche did not exist because she had never existed, because he had never dared take the step, then things were bad.

He does not look like his statue. Not even when it's melted down. It would be better to picture him as a terrified child who, with a stony face and holding all power in his hands but without knowing how to use it, stands in the midst of a sea of seething passions and says he can record and steer these passions by means of pressure points on the human body!

That was how the twentieth century began. How could it continue and end in any other manner than it did?

Blanche was afraid to abandon him.
Then he would be left all alone with his guenon Zibidie.

Occasionally there are discreet remarks about Blanche's rising fame.

She is humble, after all. Doesn't want to seem full of herself. But there are hints of growing public criticism directed toward him. Finally, his own confession in Morvan. *My experiments have now reached a dead end.*

On September 17, 1883, Charcot received a group of young Russian medical students, which included Semione Minor, Olga Tolstoy, Piotr Ivanov, and Felicia Cheftel. They were French-speaking and—to use a modern term—what might be called feminists. They were very friendly. They accused Charcot, and

the directors of the hospital, of badly mistreating the "imprisoned women." And they specifically asked about the truth of the
reports that had reached them in St. Petersburg, which claimed
that at Salpêtrière "*old-fashioned Czarist methods were used during
the hysterical crises of the women; for instance, at the onset of hysteria,
a common method was to rub the cervical area so that clotted or coagu-
lated seminal fluid would be dispersed and could then run through; this
was intended to calm the patient.*"

But Charcot assured them that such methods were used
only in special cases. His conversation with the Russian students—who nevertheless spoke French—was also devoted to
the attempts being made at the Pasteur Institute to cure Russian
farmers who had been infected with rabies, as well as to *the occurrence of hysterics and nymphomaniacs in modern novels.* The Russian
students were surprised and shocked by Charcot's friendliness
and charm. They also asked to have a brief conversation with
Charcot's famous medium, Blanche Wittman, to which Charcot
reluctantly agreed, but the medium refused to participate.

Charcot then had to comply. No conversation with
Blanche.

It's noteworthy that there was a steady stream of Russian
medical students who came to visit Charcot. Not until 1886
were they replaced by an entirely new and modern type of
young person, when the thirty-year-old Sigmund Freud joins
Charcot as his secretary and later becomes the interpreter and
proponent of Charcot's findings and ideas.

The first encounter between Freud and Charcot proceeded
quite well.

Yet certain details of Freud's description of the master reveal
how puzzled Sigmund is. Charcot greeted his assistants by
extending three fingers; his assistant physicians he greeted with
two. Sigmund makes note of the lack of rigid hierarchies,

something that differentiated Salpêtrière from the hospitals in Berlin and Vienna. He also makes note of Charcot's "democratic principles."

Sigmund Freud never really liked the Friday performances, which he found deeply fascinating. He distrusted the women. He found it detestable that they were forced to keep silent and were invited to express themselves only through their fits. Otherwise nothing but admiration. He is immediately curious about Blanche, tries to initiate a conversation with her, perhaps with sexual intentions, but fails.

She detested him, she says in the Book of Questions. She claims that it was her own findings, and to a certain extent Charcot's, about human nature, the human being's inner continent, as well as the nature of love, that were epoch-making, and that Sigmund was merely an ignorant but receptive disciple. Her arrogance is palpable, even though she may have been right. But she hated Sigmund, and later Babinski as well.

Babinski she hated with particular intensity, his cowardice, his terror of the unknown. His stab in the back of those who dared. He had tried to touch her breast; that's when she grabbed his hand and bit it.

He screamed in surprise, and she said with her usual, gentle, good-natured smile:

"Rabies, infected by the Russian peasants."

He never tried it again.

The traitors, as she calls them. The Book of Questions is, in this sense, an act of revenge and a posthumous defense of Charcot, his life, and actions *before he entered the dead-end street of love and was killed by me.*

5.

That's what it says on one of the last pages of The Yellow Book.

We have to imagine that by then she was on her way into Marie Curie's life, like an anguished mother who finds her child threatened. A child about to repeat her own mistakes, which is the worst thing of all: as if she had *given birth to the catastrophes* in the child's life.

Bore the responsibility and felt the blame and now, for that reason, with terror and alarm, was on her way out of her own story and into Marie's.

The child! The child!

In March 1910, the year before Marie Curie was awarded her second Nobel Prize, this time in chemistry, Marie came into her room, sat down on the edge of the bed, and asked what she should do.

"What's his name?" asked Blanche.

"Paul. I'm strong and he's weak, but I love him; he has to be saved from himself."

Blanche looked at Marie for a long time in silence.

Then:

"Saved from himself? Like Charcot? Then I'm frightened."

It came out in an oddly hoarse and guttural voice, like a cry for help.

Or, from the Book of Questions, after the headline **When did Marie's mental illness due to grief come to an end?** the drier comment: *Yet the anxiety that filled Marie was not as great as the joy she felt at this love, and I urgently encouraged her to show her love openly, and to everyone, not just to me. That was why, at my earnest appeal, she put on clothing that diverged from her mourning attire, and quite soon her friends began to suspect that something had happened.*

And then it started.

"Like Charcot." And then she grew frightened. Perhaps she knew what would happen, and she loved Marie.

But she was frightened.

The last pages of The Yellow Book are blank. Then comes The Black Book, more shocking, with certain pages torn out, as if in panic, or fear.

The Black Book

V

———◆———

THE SONG OF JEALOUSY

1.

THAT INCESSANT: *MARIE! MARIE! WAS IT TRULY NECESSARY?*

What a peculiar word: necessary. As if it were merely a question of what was necessary.

Not at all.

In the Book of Questions several fragments of brief, apparently meaningless, encounters between Paul and Marie, evidently recorded heedlessly or hastily by Blanche.

Paul had shown Marie the obituary for Pierre after his death and asked her what she thought.

"Very beautiful," she said. "Accurate. Very beautiful."

"I took great pains with it."

She then gave a start, as if at an insult or as if trying to restrain from voicing an objection, and inquired:

"Pains?"

"For your sake," he said, and quickly added: "For his."

"Thank you."

All those brief conversations that Marie had with Paul, and in between that terrifying silence!

2.

Why is The Black Book the one that has been torn up?

In this book there's a great deal about what led up to Marie's catastrophe. But almost nothing about Charcot other than an absurdly self-assured line: *Marie*, writes Blanche, *might never have survived if I hadn't, with my experiences from Salpêtrière and Doctor Charcot's training, if in friendship I hadn't given her the courage to face life and in this manner saved her from the inner frostbite and the scientific rigor that were about to kill her and her sanity.*

Scientific rigor!?

No doubt Blanche was trying to defend herself. And give some meaning to her terrible life. That's not so strange.

Surely we would all like to see things make sense.

We have to imagine what life was like for a female scientist at this early stage of the *fantastic and scientifically epochal* twentieth century.

What self-assurance, by the way. When did the twentieth century's self-assurance, its optimism about progress, its arrogance all disappear? When the catastrophe reached its climax for Marie Curie, the First World War, fortunately! began, and she signed up as a volunteer radiologist so as, in this way, to illuminate the torn-apart bodies of the twentieth century. Was it then, around 1914, that the twentieth century's arrogance ceased?

Poetically shaped by Marie Curie in her x-ray bus.

But before that time, to live as the female star of science! That hatred! On a clearly illuminated stage! And with the hostile wild animals all around!

And how the madness then blew apart this female star in the scientific firmament. She who had won a Nobel Prize and would soon receive another, fell in love with a married man with four children and was unwilling to give up this love! A mortal sin!

Marie, Marie. Soon it will start.

In The Black Book, Blanche records a dream that Marie had.

Marie is walking through the snow, across a plain, later an ice plain, perhaps an Arctic ice plain; she comes to a grave in the ice. Someone is buried there. The melting ice has run out across the face and then frozen; a thin membrane of ice covers the facial features of the dead man. In her dream Marie claps her hands in amazement and joy, exclaiming:

"Look, Blanche! It's me!"

Countless examples of the hatred toward successful women, especially the hatred toward *female scientists*. Even those who liked and loved Marie assumed that her coldness was a prerequisite for her genius.

Without coldness, no genius.

In June 1913, when everything is almost over and Marie has survived, although frozen, and before the liberating First World War breaks out and rescues her in an ambulance, she takes a walk with Albert Einstein in Switzerland, near Engadin. He writes to his cousin: *"Madame Curie is very intelligent, but she's as cold as a fish, which means that she has a hard time showing joy or sorrow; most often she expresses her feelings by grunting."*

Who was it she saw in the ice grave?

Marie had said that her lover Paul was drawn to her "as if to a light." Did she think of him as a moth or a bird, or a person in a dark forest? What kind of light was it that streamed out of her?

That blue gleam?

Cold as a fish. Light in a forest. A man in an ice grave, covered by a membrane of ice.

Marie had many faces.

Unexpected and, in reality, thoroughly unnecessary visits made by Paul to Marie's laboratory.

Arriving with a teapot in a basket. *But Paul! How nice!*

Standing close to her as he pours the tea. He has such beautiful hands, she suddenly sees. At night she awakes from a disturbing dream, sweat all over her body, the sheets damp. She can't go back to sleep. In the dream his hands were touching her. I'm forty-one years old, I'm still young, she tries to think. Is it too late?

Cautiously whispering into the dark:

"Blanche?"

No answer. In the next room the children are sleeping, *and they mean everything.*

"Blanche? Are you asleep?"

Marie had everything, after all. Honor, fame, children, influential friends. Then why love?

But that slowly pulsing memory! The itching! The weakness in the belly! And not directed at anyone, merely that *anonymous heat!* Those are Blanche's words, the part about the anonymous heat. But she must have heard them. Desire's lack of direction! like the compass at the North Pole! It spins around and around; if only there had been a direction!

And so sudden.

3.

The first time Marie touched him it was ten o'clock at night on March 4, 1910.

The location was a spot close to the work table in the storeroom on rue Lhomond, where the first discovery of polonium and radium had occurred more than ten years earlier, and where an experiment with piezoelectric quartz crystal waves was carried out, while Pierre was alive. The place where everything changed was a point located about a meter to the left of the table, but the point later moved to the table, and then a glass flask was broken. That was the spot, right there, she used to think. *I made note of the place with a precision that served no purpose, as if there too I were a scientist and not a woman in love.*

Later, however, she saw that table with different eyes.

Take note: Marie's words about the spot. She knows: There is always a point from which the landscape of the narrative can be regarded. If this point cannot be found, the story comes to an end.

That's the reason for Blanche's three books: the compass is spinning; if only there were a fulcrum for the lever of love!

So that the balance of the world could be upset.

In hindsight a person always sees things with different eyes. Tables are transformed and become sacred places. Several more years pass, and they're such painful places that they can't be revisited.

She had no specific intention. *It was by chance that Paul and I happened to meet on that fateful*—she should not have used the word "chance," that provocative dress was not a matter of chance, why else that excitement, the pounding heart—*that fateful day when I, for the first time, was driven to conquer my feminine shyness and he*—yes, what was it that he had conquered?

She stood there in the room and he stood next to the table at ten o'clock at night. Perhaps for a moment they shared with each other their darkness, and were overcome, causing that light to appear. And then he would wear her, *like the mine worker wears his headlamp.*

How long she had known him!

It was something about the eyes! his eyes! Sometimes they would be completely dead and extinguished, and she knew, almost certainly, that his unhappy marriage was to blame, and all those *ghastly scenes* that she had known about for a long time; then his eyes would be completely extinguished and dead.

And she recognized this.

She knew that she herself occasionally, occasionally! had that dead look, as if her face were covered with ice! But then Paul's eyes would change; he would become like a child, and frightened as a child he would then look at her with those very different eyes, as if he were an utterly alive human being.

Suddenly she saw him standing right there in the room.

The point! from which the story can be regarded and become real! one day a meter away from the table over there! while Pierre was alive! she had found the secret substance! and it became the blue radioactive light! wasn't this the proper point for conquering her fear?

She then said—it was ten o'clock at night; she reported all this later, as if Blanche's black book were a scientific journal; it happened in her laboratory, next to the table with the glass retorts—she then said:

"Paul, am I really a live human being?"

How long had she known him? Fifteen years?

He was always wrapped up in his family, or among friends; he had always smiled at her, and nothing was ever said. What was it that had slowly crept in? The allure of what was utterly forbidden? Or the glimpse of a person who was perhaps completely unique and warm and yearned for her, almost the way she had known all along that she herself yearned; and then her control was shattered. *Paul, am I a live human being?* How banal; what did the words mean? That she was dead, like a fish?

She was standing perhaps two meters away from him, and he was standing on *the spot*. And yet he must have understood.

What is it that sometimes make a person suddenly understand? *How should the living speak to the living, what words can I direct at you, whom I love, other than honed knives of silence and queries, while what should be said remains unspoken on the shore, like a seashell?* No, that poem had not been written; that was not what she said or thought; it simply happened. That was the crucial moment, as she would later realize, of her entire life.

He merely looked at her, without replying.

"Paul," she said, "I'm frightened. Sometimes I think I'm dead."

"What do you mean?"

But she couldn't explain, she simply moved closer to him, very close to him.

"I don't know what I mean," she said.

The room on that night was something she would always remember. The table. Almost no light in the room. Just that warm darkness that was alive and that made her move toward a boundary that was so enticing and palpable that she could almost touch it with her hand.

She touched him.

"This is dangerous," he said.

"I know."

"This is dangerous," he repeated.

"It doesn't matter," she replied. "It doesn't matter."

And then she kept on touching him. In that twilight.

The light was not like the kind emitted by radium; no, the light had radiated through the warm darkness, which made it possible to approach *that spot where he stood and where it was possible to survey her life*. It was warm and not deadly, although filled with terror and desire, and suddenly there was no turning back.

He kissed her, she was pressed against the table, she threw out her arm.

She heard the sound of glass breaking.

She cleared off the table with a single sweep of her hand. His eyes were no longer those of a child and no longer dead; no, now they were like the eyes of an utterly alive human being. *Paul*, she whispered and knew that it was now, *Paul, this isn't dangerous*, and he flung aside her dress and lifted her up onto the table where once *someone*, no, she was the one! alone! first measured radium, and that's where discoveries were made that would change history. Now she was very close to another discovery, she was resolute and warm. His eyes had given up the terrified defense that she thought she saw; she knew that he loved her very much, perhaps beyond a boundary that until now he had not dared cross, everything was very warm and dark and she knew all of a sudden that his darkness and hers were melting together. She merely said, *oh, slowly! cautiously!* and slowly he pushed his way inside her.

Shards of glass were still on the table. It didn't hurt.

She came almost at once, in gentle rhythmic thrusts, and she was not afraid to come, and then she understood that he too had crossed the last boundary of fear, and he too came inside her, this woman whom he had desired for almost fifteen years, desired night and day, this Marie who had been the most forbidden, deadly, and the most desired. She was the one who raised her hand to touch his cheek, and lowered her hand to touch his sex, which was as hard as his sex had been in his dreams ever since he first set eyes on her. But had not taken, had not dared, Marie, the one who was most forbidden and thus mortally threatening, whom he loved, though he had always known that *he who touches Marie touches death*, and that's why she possessed this insane allure.

That was how it began.

Afterward he had placed her on the floor and sat down at her side and both of them knew that it was inescapable.

"Is it starting now?" she asked.

Why did she say that? He didn't reply.

Toward morning, around one o'clock, Marie returned to her apartment, went into Blanche's room, woke her up, and told her everything.

She had bloodstains on her back because the shards of glass on the table had been pressed into her back. She took off her dress and tossed it into a corner. The glass cuts were superficial; Blanche bathed them in alcohol. Marie was very calm.

"Who is he, actually?" asked Blanche, even though she knew who he was, but not in this sense.

"That's something the future will show," replied Marie.

Blanche took note of her immense calm.

"That's something the future will show," she then repeated, but her face was so calm that no one could hear or comprehend that the words meant something else. She had been waiting almost her whole life to speak them: nothing about terror or boundaries, nothing about the most forbidden or this deadly allure; something much simpler and more terrifying: *Marie! Marie! And she took off!*

4.

So who was he?

It may not be possible to summarize the truth but to give instead *the general opinion* in Paris about his and Marie's situation, for example as it was in the autumn of 1910, and without any exaggeration and as an accurate summary of what was written in the public sector, say that his name was Paul Langevin, he was an honorable French researcher and father of four whose marriage and happy French family life were destroyed by a foreign woman whose maiden name was Skłodowska, a woman who was perhaps of Jewish birth! Jewish! which had to be regarded as a further attack on all things *French* after the national and tragic defeat of Dreyfus the Jew, and the victory of the accusers of Dreyfus the Jew!

Yes, she was undoubtedly a Jewess! Why else would her middle name be Salomea?

A foreign, and perhaps Jewish, woman who in that case had hidden and denied her Jewish birth and perhaps was basically someone who *in the area of morals was just as guilty as Dreyfus was in the military arena!!!* as one newspaper later claimed, and like him was certainly guilty.

But at any rate, she was Polish.

And it was perfectly clear that this foreign Skłodowska, who through marriage had acquired the French name of Curie, it was perfectly clear that she was not merely a woman but a blasphemous intellectual with contacts in emancipated circles, for example with those in England! the notorious suffragettes! with whom she consorted. A woman who, when her scandalous behavior was exposed, tried to hide from the public but was finally forced to come forward, in the press, in public, and suffer the public shame that she deserved; later, for example, in connection with "the scandalous awarding to her of a second Nobel Prize," a prize she did not deserve and which, in a way, ended her affair with the basically innocent Paul Langevin.

Something like that.

So who was he?

In 1907 Paul made his greatest and most unique contribution to physics: this was his application of the electron theory to the phenomenon of magnetism; basically it was an explanation of the magnetism experiment that Pierre Curie had conducted in 1895.

He brought together the experiments of Thomson and Curie,

giving them an explanation. He was the type of person who could see a connection but could never find on his own the root of what was inexplicable; that was why Marie always despaired on his behalf. He brought together diverse circles but was scorned because he could never create anything unique or make sense of anything unique.

Paul, Marie used to say to her friends as she wept, *never receives the respect he deserves, he's a synthesizer.*

He himself accepted his lot without tears.

But over time, at least, he did become very well known.

During the First World War, Paul Langevin's work with the phenomenon of piezoelectricity, which was used to produce sound waves with a high frequency, made it possible with sonar and echo-sound to locate the enemy's submarines, and in this respect it represented a significant contribution to the war. He didn't believe himself capable of falling in love, but he was struck by an illness by the name of Marie Curie which he knew could never be cured. Yet by 1895 he had already become a doctoral candidate and researcher at the Cavendish Laboratory along with Ernest Rutherford. It is this Rutherford who walks three paces behind Marie and Paul one night in 1903 in the garden in Paris when a wand, half coated with zinc sulfide and containing a solution of radium, glows brightly in the dark, and Marie suddenly turns to Paul and sees that his eyes are alive; *it was a magnificent finale to an unforgettable day*

But he had noticed Marie much earlier.

Pierre Curie was Paul Langevin's teacher at the École de physique et chimie back in 1888, when Paul was seventeen. He meets Marie soon after Pierre and Marie's wedding in 1895. He admires his teacher Pierre. He is respectful. Pierre has achieved everything; Pierre's exclusive property is also the holy grail that is Marie's body. She is the holy grail.

Whoever touches the holy grail must die; he knows that. It's the secret of love and its innermost driving force.

He is convinced that the philosophers of the Enlightenment were right in believing that the pursuit of happiness is the unique privilege of human beings; but since Marie, for him, is the only possible happiness and he is forbidden to pursue, the theory falls apart. He starts thinking of her as "the inevitability of the human tragedy." That doesn't make it any easier. He regards his teacher's wife as a symbol of the impossibility of love. Paul then becomes Marie's colleague; that's later, the years pass. She can be found close, very close to him. The impossible haunts him.

He feels himself shrinking.

How excruciating that she is so near. What is unattainable should not be so near that it can be touched. Marie is moving close to him but at an infinite distance. As his admiration for Pierre grows, something else increases; is it the distance? is it merely a longing for the grail? or hatred?

At first he speaks to Marie with deference, later with collegial familiarity, later almost with anger. *Marie, Marie, where is this heading? so beautiful, so impossible to touch, so soft.*

"Paul is an extraordinary nuclear physicist; he believes in ions as if they were a religion!" his teacher Pierre says patronizingly. Doesn't a person have to hate such patronizing, such friendliness? Paul is also a republican, critical of the French educational system, and he hates hierarchies; he signed Zola's petition in 1898 in support of Dreyfus, which makes the outrage in the press in connection with the Curie scandal even murkier.

Perhaps Paul deserved his foreign woman? *his possible Jewess?* Perhaps that was the way things had to turn out?

Once in the autumn of 1901 she places her hand on his. She does it again in March 1903. And smiles!

That's while Pierre is alive. A *friendly smile.* Paul becomes tremendously excited, imagines for a long time that hand, how it touches his naked body.

Her hand! And yet it's deformed! But he disregards the radiation damage on that hand. The hand takes the place of her body: that white, voluptuous, utterly unattainable body. If only once in his life he might empty himself into that body! which belongs, belongs! to his admired teacher and mentor. Marie, Marie, where is this heading?

What is the chemical formula for desire?

And why isn't there any standard meter for love? Why does love constantly change, quite unlike the standard meter, that ten-millionth of the earth's meridian quadrant? Why is there no atomic weight for desire, confirmed, awarded with a prize, for everyone, for all time, forever?

Half a page in The Black Book. Torn off. The question: **Why like a branding iron on an animal?**

The beginning of the answer: *Once when Paul was visiting, Marie playfully invited him to dance in the kitchen, and for several minutes she pressed herself so close to him, in spite of the fact that she was menstruating at the time, that he*

The rest has been torn off. Had she provoked him? Did she know that on sleepless nights he would relive these seconds, as in an eternity of sexuality, as if he were forever marked, *like a branding iron on an animal?*

Why the comment about menstruation?

When Pierre Curie died, it was Paul Langevin who wrote the best and most insightful obituary. Marie liked it very much. He was the one who understood.

Paul *had taken great pains.*

He tried to interpret Marie. He thought that she had many faces. Marie spent time, *unpretentiously,* with Paul and his wife Jeanne Langevin and their four children. Marie is concerned when Jeanne complains about her husband's brusque manner. She is outraged! when she learns that Jeanne smashed a bottle on her husband's head. She takes note of the "ghastly behavior" of the spouses. Yet none of this indicates that a love affair is about to destroy Marie's life; she is concerned for him, he ostensibly plays an unimportant role.

But the sound of the ticking time bomb of love? Nothing like that?

Perhaps. Yet in Blanche's Book of Questions only scattered and curious notes about Paul up until the spring of 1910, only hesitant notes—(menstruation!)—indicate that he is about to play a role.

He is reposing, secure and painless like a cancerous tumor of love, in her life.

Blanche is also awaiting her time. It will come.

In her Book of Questions Blanche reports on long nightly conversations between herself and Marie, but the conversations are devoted solely to Salpêtrière, to the women there, and to the doctors. Marie seems increasingly gripped with fascination by what Blanche recounts. She wants to know more, about the experiments, about the attacks, about the escapes.

What is she thinking about?

But no one knows what Paul was thinking about. His wife Jeanne could hear him breathing in the dark; he was not asleep. It was in the dark that Marie became most visible. She would come through the dark like a shimmering blue glow, yes, that's how he liked to think of it, *as if the dark were irradiated by Marie;* he breathed so hard, so hard that Jeanne Langevin asked in a whisper, night after night:

"Paul? What are you thinking about? Are you asleep?"
But he did not answer.

5.

Marie said: We have to be practical. He asked her what she meant; she said *we have to be practical,* we have to rent an apartment that is all our own.

And so on July 15, 1910, they rented an apartment, a two-room place, at rue Banquier, number 5. That's where they could meet. The apartment was sparsely furnished, though it did have a sofa and chair upholstered in light green fabric. Marie discovered to her surprise that she was very pleased with that sofa and chair, and especially the green color, which reminded her of *a summer meadow in Zakopane.*

The bedroom was very plain: a bed.

Paul had not done much; if anything he was astonished at the practical matter-of-factness displayed by Marie, but he was basically happy. His first little notes to Marie are filled with an almost carefree joy. The grail is his, and he hasn't realized what that means. *I'm writing in all haste to say that if you don't show up in the morning, I'll come back to our nest in the afternoon, after two. I long impatiently to see you, much more than I worry about all the difficulties ahead. It will be marvelous to hear your voice again and to look into your wondrous eyes. I will try to figure out some kind of acceptable living situation for the two of us, and I agree with you as to what is required for this to become a reality.*

Everything seemed so simple.

Marie could walk through the streets to their apartment *chez nous,* and it wasn't far; she could walk briskly and feel that nothing was strenuous, *she could walk a thousand miles and carry the sorrows of Poland on her shoulders and not even begin to breathe hard*—the quote is astonishing because it's the only time in her conversations with Blanche that she mentions *the sorrows of her homeland.* She could meet Paul in the doorway and embrace him and slowly, matter-of-factly, and with a smile start to undress him, and not for a moment either notice or take into consideration his shyness.

She had once described the Polish oppression, meaning the oppression of Polish culture and Polish freedom, as a primordial force resembling repressed love.

He wanted to make love in the dark, but she lit a candle. The sounds from the street did not disturb them, except for one time when she, as they made love, and with her eyes suddenly wide with terror, thought she heard *the rumbling sound of a nine-meter flatbed wagon weighing six tons and with a driver by the name of Manin, as it swung around the corner at such a great speed that Marie, with a cry of surprise or terror, happened to break off their love interlude, although without explaining why to her lover.* One time she was lying on the bed naked when he arrived; he stopped in the doorway and regarded her, almost in shock. She said: Come in! You're not dreaming! It's me! He stepped over to the bed and fell to his knees and began to cry. Don't cry, she said, but cry if that's what you want to do.

"Just imagine if it comes to an end," he said.

Perhaps the fact that the apartment was so secret and forbidden made her feel free.

Afterwards she could lie completely still and look up at the ceiling and study the flickering shadows from the burning candle and know that *many times the members of the Polish resistance would hide in apartments like this one, and there they would carry on their discussions about the survival of the Polish language and culture.* It's clear that she must have seen the difference; their love nest was quite different from a hideout for the resistance, although maybe not? Maybe not for her? There was something warm and secretive about the forbidden apartment that made her feel as if

she were swimming in a warm ocean, being rocked in warm
water; no, as if she were resting, enveloped by a membrane, like
a fetus in the womb? Was it possible to think like that? Wasn't
this fetus resting inside a life-giving amniotic fluid? She convinced herself that at the same time what she was experiencing
was something greater: the innermost meaning of life, revealed
only to innocent children.

As it is to me, she thought.

She tried to tell him about this, but she knew that he
wouldn't understand what it was like to live in exile, which
meant that you were always driven to search for a kind of womb,
in the midst of life, wherever you happened to be!

As if you were always trying to go home to that womb. Did
he understand? Wherever you happened to be! always!

She had brought bedclothes from her own apartment, carrying them in a basket, the way a market woman carries her
eggs.

Each day she would carry this egg basket of cleanliness to
their love bed. Why do you do that? he asked. Someone might
notice and start asking questions. She replied: One day someone
is bound to notice and start asking questions. Don't you realize
that? He would often fall asleep, and she would gaze with love at
his face, the way all the sharp edges would dissolve, becoming shy
and childish. This is where we've moved, in here, into the innermost exile, *we're resting in the womb of Europe,* she once told him.

He found that amusing, though a bit affected, and so she
didn't ever repeat it.

Since everything they did was forbidden, she was no longer
afraid of anything. I'm not very experienced, she once said;
everything they did when they made love surpassed her experience and was new. What is the meaning of experience? she
asked. It's done with, and dead matter. You're a physicist, she said,

the universe exists in the atom that is this bed, don't believe in anything, why are you afraid?

"I'm not afraid," he repeated, perhaps a few times too often for her to believe him.

She refused to be afraid. Or for him to be afraid. In that way she wanted to *take him with her.* That's why she told him about the journey to Nome.

It turned out to be a big mistake. But how was she to know?

At first she was afraid that he would think she was experienced. Later she was no longer afraid. Don't worry, she told him. Surely we can pretend that we met by chance, and that you're on your way to some town in Alaska, never to return. What are some towns in Alaska? he asked. Nome, I think, she replied. It's not in Greenland, at any rate, he said. All the better, she said. You're headed for Nome and will stay just one night in Paris and later, on the journey to Nome, you die. And no one can harm you, and we've had such a splendid time.

Why do I have to die? So that neither of us will be terror-stricken on that night in Paris.

And later we imagine the same thing, night after night, for an eternity of eternities. You walk across an endless ice plain and die before you reach Nome. Why do I have to die? Because otherwise you would be frightened by what we're doing in Paris. No one knows anything, no one will ever know. We too have forgotten. It has all been erased.

Imagine that. It has been erased, everything before and after that night, and later, in the eternity of eternities, you dare to do anything, and I dare to do anything. Picture yourself traveling to Nome. And you will never, ever see me again, and I never have to be ashamed before anyone, since you die on the journey to Nome.

He didn't understand.

It made him upset, that's the whole truth. But when she told him about his journey to Nome she had somehow felt freer, maybe even completely free. They made love. It was better than ever before, and better than it would ever be again. But she realized that he didn't really care for the story about Nome.

"You want me to die," he said then, almost matter-of-factly, speaking straight into the dark room, where the candle had long since burned out and night had fallen and the sounds from the street had almost ceased.

She protested vigorously and asked him how he could say something so stupid, as if he doubted her love.

"It won't help if I die in Nome," he then replied.

Three weeks later he returned to the subject, as if he had merely interrupted what he'd been thinking and was now continuing:

"Do you remember the journey to Nome? It won't help. Jeanne is suspicious. She must have heard something."

"Are you afraid?"

But he didn't have to reply because she already knew the answer.

6.

When it's right, you shouldn't speak, she thought whenever it was best.

What she meant was merely: that when it was best he would lie completely still and quiet inside her, and she would feel how his member almost imperceptibly moved inside her; and you shouldn't think! You should just be enveloped in the midst of life. That's how it should be. And quiet, like a dog's muzzle! like the dog she had had as a child! Then they should sniff at each other, inside of her, but without thinking! It should be as if their mucous membranes sniffed, cautiously, at each other, as if his member were the muzzle of a dog that was shyly licking her cervix.

When it was good, it was like that.

She didn't want to explain it in words because he always misunderstood her words. When it was best, it was without words. He was deep inside her, quiet but at the same time curious; and she was not thinking of anything at all. All thoughts had been erased; that was what she meant with the icy trek to Nome. No history and no punishment and no guilt, above all no guilt! no guilt! All her thoughts should be gathered around the muzzle of the dog, which was curious and very loving. Why was it so difficult to explain to him how it ought to be, when he could understand everything about radiation and physics?

But not the part about Nome.

She didn't dare say that all her membranes and muscles and all her warmth and all her freedom and everything else were gathered there, deep inside her; and she hardly moved at all when it was best.

When it was best it was almost completely quiet.

Then they would lie quietly. It would never end; they were surrounded by and enveloped by each other. It would never end because that was how love should be: like a pause on the journey to Nome, that one single moment, and curiously and cautiously like the dog's muzzle, that's how it should be, *forever and outside of reality, but only on that one night.*

That's how she thought of love. That's what she meant with that journey to Nome, that there was no after or before, and at any rate nothing outside of their little shared space. And then he uttered that line about *Jeanne has become suspicious.*

It was almost like treason.

7.

Looking back, it seems incomprehensible that Marie's brief happiness lasted only six months. From March 1910 until August 1910. Then everything turned so ugly that nothing could have been completely repaired, even though the definitive explosion didn't come until November 1911.

After that she would never be able to approach a man, find a lover, start over. Six months.

Suddenly everything turned much uglier.

It was wonderful as long as it lasted, for almost six months, but when things turned ugly, they were truly ugly. A number of testimonies suddenly appeared that recounted, with varying degrees of outrage or glee, how *Jeanne had truly become suspicious* and refused to hide it, and wanted to take action and kill.

That was love too; or at least hers. In the story Jeanne is nearly invisible. I assume that she also has a story, that she also lay in bed and stared at the ceiling.

If all the stories are placed on top of each other, everything ultimately becomes invisible. Then you have to choose.

A letter from Marie to Paul had been fished out of a mailbox by a maid and given to Madame Langevin. That was the proof.

Professor Jean Perrin, who was friends with both Marie and Paul and knew about the situation, had paid a visit to Jeanne Langevin and tried to calm her down, but she firmly insisted that she would kill that Polish whore, that interloper in their marriage. At any rate she was going to inform the French press.

A few days later Perrin came home late one evening, and outside his house, to his immense surprise, he found the Nobel Prize winner Marie Curie, who came running to meet him across the boulevard. Marie had been waiting for several hours, sitting on the wall outside his house, and she now told him that she had been *accosted by Madame Langevin and her sister Madame Bourgeois and showered with the most vulgar insults, and the furious woman had threatened her and shouted at her to "leave France and go back home."*

Marie looked like "a hunted animal." She was at her wits' end.

The next day Professor Perrin went to see Madame Langevin, to act as mediator. She then demanded that Marie leave the country within a week; otherwise she would be murdered.

It was ugly. It would get even uglier. No purpose would be served by traveling to Nome.

What should I do? she asked Blanche.

But Blanche had no advice to offer; Blanche had lived in a different world, which was in some ways uglier, but in others not at all ugly in that sense.

Go away, she told her. Leave Paris. It's dangerous to stay here.

But where should I go? asked Marie.

Not to Nome, Blanche replied.

8.

She ended up choosing L'Arcouest.

It was the first flight from love that she would undertake. All the previous flights had been attacks. But this was definitely a flight.

L'Arcouest was a little fishing village on the coast of Brittany. It consisted of a handful of houses that stood jammed between the rocky precipice and the sea. The rocks were red. You could walk along the shore and gaze out at the sea. A woman who was in despair and had seen her lover hesitate could simply walk along the shore in the storm, or the next day sit alone on a pier as the waves rolled in and the rain fell harder. Marie knew that she had to make a decision, and she could not afford to hesitate. Who could she talk to?

Blanche sat in her wooden box back home in Paris.

She later recalled her days in L'Arcouest as a period inside an ice grave, that's how she expressed it, but she is not dead, nor is she covered with a membrane of ice, and she knows what's at stake but can find no solution.

It is then, in August 1910, that she writes the letter to Paul that would become the catastrophe of her life.

Marie, Marie, why did you write it?

Oh, it's so easy to ask that question: Why did she write it? Why that candor, why that knack for practical matters, why that friendly crudeness, why that cynicism, why that tremendous determination to hold on to her lover? Why did you write that letter, Marie? As if she didn't know that Paul was weak. As if it were possible to make him brave and strong and the one who could withstand storms, even those that might surge up around someone who was now a world-famous female Nobel Prize winner, the first! surrounded by so much admiration and hatred, not in the least someone who, with her clothes dirty, weeping and confused, runs across the boulevard one night toward a friend by the name of Perrin and says that everything is dreadful and that she's going to die and that a scandal is unavoidable. That this world-famous woman is now about to lose all prestige and that everything will instantly, in one second! be transformed from respect to contempt.

Falling might not be so difficult, but to fall from such heights! so far! and the children! and the shame!

Then she writes a letter to Paul which says that all is not lost.

But that insufferable pragmatic tone! That almost pedagogical, didactic tone! *Your wife lacks the ability to keep her composure and allow you to have your freedom; she will always try to exert control over you, for all sorts of reasons: material advantages, restlessness, and why not ordinary laziness, and don't forget that the two of you disagree about everything having to do with the children's education and the running of the household; all the same sort of quarrels that have plagued you ever since you got married and which are quite foreign to me.*

She reminds him of his misery, so matter-of-factly! that tremendously matter-of-fact tone! it's insufferable; but isn't there something else as well?

The instinct that led us to each other must have been enormously strong, since it helped us to conquer so many misunderstandings about what we both realized would be the different way in which our private life would take shape. And what might arise from this feeling, so instinctive and spontaneous, and yet so compatible with our intellectual needs. I think we should be able to derive everything from this affinity: a rewarding work relationship, security and tenderness, the courage to face life, and with wonderful love-children in the most beautiful sense of the word.

So far merely an ordinary love letter. But it goes on.

This is no cold fish speaking, no scientific analyst, no burning revolutionary, no suffragette, no gentle beloved wife, no guarded public figure, and no admired Nobel Prize winner who is a role model for women all over the world. It's Marie, an animal in a hostile jungle, and a human being fighting for her life, with no holds barred. *There is no question of your wife readily agreeing to a separation, since she has nothing to win by doing so; the whole goal of her life has been to exploit you, and she will see only disadvantages in such a solution. What is worse, it is in her nature to hold on tight if she has any inkling that you would rather she left you.*

And so, no matter how difficult it is for you, it is essential that you decide to do everything in your power to make life intolerable for her, methodically and single-mindedly.

If she says that she will go along with a separation if she gets to keep the children, then you have to accept the proposal without hesitation so that you can put a stop to the blackmail that she will otherwise attempt. For the time being, it's sufficient that Jean continues as a boarder at school and that you live at EPCI in Paris; you can go out to Fontenay to visit the other children or see to it that they come to the Perrin home; the change shouldn't be as overwhelming as you think, and it would certainly be better for all concerned. We can continue taking the same precautionary measures as we do now whenever we meet, until everything has calmed down. And it goes on and on and on.

She wants to rescue him and she wants to own him and she has been gripped by the mortal sickness of love that is not beautiful, not always. *You must do everything in your power to make life intolerable for her, methodically and single-mindedly.*

It is not beautiful. But for the first time in her life she is seized by a love that sweeps everything else aside: and the whole time that ghastly thought that the other one, the hated one, will dupe him into returning to his lawful bed, to sex, and perhaps ensure that she becomes pregnant.

And that would exclude Marie for good.

One of the first things you must do is take back your own room. It makes me uneasy because I can't prepare you for what might happen. I'm frightened about the fits of weeping that you have such a hard time steeling yourself against, and the traps that will entice you to get her pregnant; you have to mistrust all those sorts of things. I beg you, don't make me wait long to know that you have separate sleeping arrangements. Only then can I endure the steps toward your separation with less anxiety. Don't ever come down from your bedroom upstairs, work late, and if you need some pretext, say that you need your rest because you're working late into the night and have to get up early, that you're upset by her demand to share a bed and that it would be impossible for you to get the proper rest.

Yes, it's excruciating. Marie, Marie, it's excruciating.

She is tormented by her thoughts, and there is a sword slicing through her body; the fantasies and images dance through her mind, it hurts! hurts! hurts! *and if you happen to have given in out of sheer exhaustion during the holidays, you must now refuse to let it continue, and if she insists, then you need to stay in Paris overnight with Jean*; no, it may not be beautiful, but despair is seldom beautiful.

And she knows that. And then she concludes, in quiet despair. *But as long as I know that you're with her I have to endure horrible nights; I can't sleep. With great difficulty I manage to doze off for two or three hours; I awake in a fever and I cannot work. Do what you can to put an end to this.*

Marie wrote a very long letter that is an ugly and gripping portrait of love the way it is sometimes. Yet in reality it's quite splendid. But in any case not suited for publication in a French newspaper the following autumn, in *L'Œuvre* on November 23, 1911. The letter that brought the rumbling against Marie to a climax, the storm against "*the foreign woman who destroyed a French family, a new Dreyfus affair, although in a new guise. But it no longer splits France in half, it shows that France is in the hands of a mob of filthy foreigners who are plundering, corrupting, and disgracing our country. Now Israel is mobilizing all its Levites, hired murderers and thugs.*"

Marie, Marie, where is it all heading?

I often think about Pasqual Pinon and his Maria.

In the freak show he met a woman by the name of Ann, and they fell in love. Maria, the female head that he wore like a miner wears his headlamp, had then, in despair and fury, begun to *sing horribly.*

Not a word crossed her lips; she had no vocal cords, after all. But she sang horribly, a stridently caustic song that was inaudible to everyone except Pasqual, and the song pierced right through him. In the end he went mad and tried to take his own life. They found him in a canyon south of Santa Barbara, seriously wounded, lying in a dried-out creek bed. He was unconscious. Maria's eyes were open wide, as if in terror or relief. She was no longer singing horribly. Four men carried Pasqual and his Maria back.

I often think about that "horrible singing." How it might have been. Some sort of ugly, stridently shrill and piercing despair; that was no doubt how the helpless Maria felt as she sat like a mute headlamp on Pasqual's head and could do nothing, nothing at all except sing horribly.

That, more or less, must be the horrible song of jealousy.

9.

Paul received the letter, read the letter, and sent a proper, friendly, somewhat impersonal reply. He read her letter once and then twice, he writes, but didn't have time to reply in detail. To the extent that he's still able to judge the situation, he too thinks that "a separation would be best," although preferably without a fight.

No doubt he was a little frightened.

A few months earlier, Marie was recommended for a chair at the Academy of Sciences.

It was an unprecedented proposal, deeply shocking, but there were only three Nobel Prize winners alive in France. Marie was one of them, and she accepted the nomination. She lost the election, and the tidal waters won, the flood of hatred rose, and "by confirming to the newspapers that she was a candidate, she has revealed a lack of modesty that is unbefitting of her gender. The public has shown hostility toward the candidate."

An oddly suppressed rage was growing toward Marie Curie.

As yet no one knew everything about her secrets. Not about the appallingly candid letter from Marie to Paul, the letter that was a horrible song about love.

But soon. By the very next autumn.

Then, one year later, came the turning point. Blanche writes in her Book of Questions under the heading When did I find out about Marie's dilemma? that at five o'clock in the evening Marie came rushing into her room, and threw herself to her knees next to Blanche's mobile wooden box. Her face was deathly pale and her hair in disarray; she did not sob but expressed the greatest despair and resignation, and gave this account.

A break-in had occurred at the love nest shared by Marie and Paul. Someone had broken down the door, searched the apartment, and stolen the letters that Marie had written to Paul.

Among them was also the long letter she had written from L'Arcouest in August 1910. Now Jeanne knew that she had a weapon, a letter that was a character assassination in the eyes of the rigid French public, or a suicide by Marie. The very next day Madame Langevin informed her attorney that she "possessed definitive proof" of Marie's infamy, proof that she would not hesitate to use in court proceedings and would allow to be published unless Marie immediately left the country and stopped subjecting her family to her scandalous presence.

That was more or less it. Marie was much too upset to take note of the threat. What she knew was that Jeanne now had in her possession a bomb, meaning a letter that could ruin forever Marie's reputation, and that she wouldn't hesitate to use it.

She was truly singing a horrible song. And that night Marie sat mute and calm next to Blanche, rocking back and forth like a forlorn child, and the whole time she kept whispering that now she had lost him.

What could anyone possibly say to console her?

Toward morning, Marie lay down on the floor and fell asleep. She was like a hunted animal; now she had been caught. She asked Blanche what she would have done in her place, but Blanche did not reply.

Yet she thought that Marie had suddenly become like a child who had hurt herself badly and could no longer cry but wanted only to lie on her mother's lap and at last whispered: tell me a story. What sort of story should I tell you? Tell me about love so I can understand. Tell me how it was, and how it ought to be. It's not something a person can understand, Blanche whispered in her ear in reply; love cannot be understood.

From love can come light, or darkness. The lovers can share their light, or their darkness; from this then comes life or death. It cannot be understood.

Tell me about Salpêtrière, Marie then said on that night, tell me so that I will survive this night too, and perhaps all other nights, for an eternity of eternities, perhaps on the way to Nome, yes, on the way to Nome.

Amor Omnia Vincit was how Blanche then could have begun, but she did not.

VI

———•—

THE SONG OF
THE BUTTERFLY

1.

THERE IS ACTUALLY A PHOTOGRAPH OF BLANCHE.

In the third volume of the gigantic photo inventory of
Charcot's patients, or perhaps it should be called a female theater ensemble, *Iconographie photographique de la Salpêtrière*, one photograph of Blanche Wittman can be found.

It's true: she is beautiful.

She has a white ruffle around her neck, like the one my
maternal grandmother Johanna wore in the photograph that I
used for my novel *The Musicians' Procession*, the one in which she
has round eyeglasses and her hair is pulled back, the one that has
gradually supplanted the funeral photo, my memory of her as a
dead person. A beautiful and strong woman. Yet Blanche doesn't
look as stern or self-assured as Johanna Lindgren. Blanche is
looking down, obliquely, to the left; she too has her hair pulled
back, but a few wispy curls have come loose, snakes freed as on
Medusa's head, and her very beautiful eyes are sorrowful.

A slender waist and soft sensual body, I write on a piece of paper
that I rediscover much later. It could apply to Blanche or Marie
Curie, but not to Johanna. Why did I think that was important?

Blanche's hands, which at the time the photograph was taken in 1880 had not yet been amputated, are clasped.

Marie can be found in even more pictures.

So beautiful and forbidden!

In the famous painting depicting the session with Blanche and Charcot, which still hangs in the library at Salpêtrière, her face is seen obliquely, in three-quarter profile.

Our attention is drawn to the spectators' faces, which are jealously curious, almost greedy. They are sharing an experience with us. Everyone sees: the motion of a falling body and the feminine resignation in Blanche.

Loneliness and jealousy.

Surrender, her blouse unbuttoned. Charcot turned toward the spectators as if with a commanding or punitive gesture. And then Babinski, who was so hated by Blanche, behind her. He opens his arms, like a Savior.

In the photograph from *Iconographie*, on the other hand, Blanche is alone, her beauty undisturbed by the glances of others, her beautiful clothing is not torn open or low-cut. No jealous onlookers. This is an alluring woman from the nineteenth century, one with great integrity.

Earrings, long ones. Expensive clothes? Yes, perhaps. No girl from the slums, but rather a sorrowful, beautiful woman with her life ahead of her. Is it like a painting? "The Lacemaker" by Vermeer? No, but I recognize her.

Someone who has her life ahead of her.

If we look at the two images of Blanche from that time—the saint and the powerless young star of Charcot's ensemble in front of the jealous spectators—if we look at her with rational eyes, she is incomprehensible.

But don't do that!

In his book *The Story of San Michele*, Axel Munthe recounts how he once witnessed a session at Salpêtrière. A performance in a large hall—he may have exaggerated, since it was customary for the room to hold only about thirty spectators.

Perhaps he wanted to magnify his experience of what he calls hypnotism, the preliminary stage to Charcot's hysteria experiments with Blanche. He saw Blanche. He never mentions her by name. That's good.

That's splendid! He doesn't besmirch her with his presence!

Doctor Munthe is filled with contempt.

"*The huge auditorium was filled to the very last seat by a diverse audience enticed from all of Paris, authors, journalists, famous actors and actresses, fashionable demimondes, all morbidly curious to witness the strange phenomenon of hypnotism. Some of the subjects of the experiments were without doubt influenced by genuine suggestions presented to them during sleep as posthypnotic suggestions. Many more of them were impostors who knew what was expected of them. Some would sniff with pleasure at a bottle of ammonia when they were told it was eau-de-cologne; others would eat a piece of charcoal when it was given to them as chocolate. Another would crawl around the floor on all fours, barking furiously, when she was told that she was a dog, or flap her arms as if attempting to fly when she was supposed to be a dove, or lift up her skirts with a cry of fear when it was suggested to her that a glove tossed on the floor was a snake. Another walked around cradling a top hat in her arms when they told her it was her child. Hypnotized right and left, dozens of times a day, by doctors and students, many of these girls spent their days in a semi-trance state, their brains bewildered by the most unreasonable suggestions, only half conscious and certainly not responsible for their actions, condemned, sooner or later, to end up in the Salles des Agités, if not the insane asylum.*"

*   *   *

I recognize this.

When I was a child, talked like a child, and had childish thoughts, meaning at the age of sixteen, I once went to a performance arranged by an artist of suggestions, a hypnotist. It was at the auditorium in Skellefteå. There were maybe seventy people in the hall. We had all paid the admission price of three kronor. I was shy, and for that reason wasn't very eager to go up on stage as a subject for the experiment, but I steeled myself, out of curiosity.

It was the first time I stood on a stage.

No, don't misunderstand me. I was not admitted to a gigantic hospital in Paris, I didn't find myself among fashionable demimondes, famous actors or avaricious intellectual observers; no, it was just the lecture hall of Skellefteå High School. There were probably six of us standing on the stage.

The hypnotist was a man of about fifty. He was sweating.

Everything that Axel Munthe described in his book *The Story of San Michele* also happened here. Perhaps not as successfully or dramatically, but the amateur hypnotist and itinerant suggestivist—is there such a word?—made an attempt. And I recall with painful clarity how I later convinced myself that I did everything for his sake. Because he was sweating so heavily. In order to assuage his fear. Because of the terror he communicated to me. Because the audience down below was a hostile mob that at any moment would have turned against him if he failed, and then it would have been my fault! I suddenly understood that! They would have turned against this dubious itinerant suggestion-artist with scorn or displeasure, like an aggressive, hostile animal, a skeptical, bloodthirsty mob that in the next second would have gone on the attack. And those of us up there—in the clear, cold electric light that made him sweat so heavily, not because of the light but above all because of fear—all of us had to demonstrate responsibility, an artistic complicity. And we had a task with regard to the hostile, mistrustful mob of people down there who might, if we failed, with a roar of scorn or laughter throw themselves upon us.

We, artists, against the beast of the crowd; and I knew that together we had to complete this terrifying and horrifying task.

Since then I have never stood on a stage, and yet I've always stood there.

The sense of solidarity in the seduction is the only thing I remember. I liked him. Before I went up on stage he was a detestable charlatan; yet up there I felt a sympathy, I shared his terror of the hostile human-beast.

That was my brief sojourn in Salpêtrière, a hospital located on the stage of the auditorium in Skellefteå High School, where I paid the three kronor entrance fee and became an accomplice.

2.

At night she would tell stories to Marie, like an amputated and motionless Scheherezade, to give some meaning to life.

Blanche Wittman's terrible life, contrary to better judgment, is presented in the three books as meaningful. Enveloped in a weak, shimmering blue light, they are each other's supplicants. *My fate, and everything that befell me under the secure supervision of Professor Charcot, often seemed to offer a form of solace to Marie.*

Her handwriting is clear, easy to read.

Level-headed recollections, interrupted by sudden, incomprehensible flights into dreams *to save Marie's life.* Then she had to put things together in a particular way. It had to make sense and have meaning. Pitchblende kills even if pine needles from a forest are mixed with it. *Radiation is making my body disintegrate. I'm not afraid. I'm going to die soon.* It occurs like a sudden, almost playful remark.

She did not say this to Marie. But perhaps she did say the following?

The explanation is certainly not that I felt fear or a sense of inferiority with regard to Charcot. On October 3, 1880, he sketched for the first time his scientific diagram on my body, which he partially uncovered, but not in an indecent manner so as to expose my breasts. The convulsions that I had suffered for many years, and that were not to be confused with epilepsy but that flung my body in an arc toward the darkening heavens, which lacked mercy, caused me to hiss as if with hatred or contempt at the God who did not exist. He punished me as if I were Job, not a butterfly that had escaped from heaven but a fallen angel subjected to vengeance. Charcot then prepared a rectangular road map in which he placed coordinates—I later learned the significance of the term—with specific designated points. He used a pen. I noticed that he did not select the points of desire that are usually viewed as having a connection with passion. When I later assisted with the work on Iconographie Photographique de la Salpêtrière, *it was almost with humorous interest that I was allowed to designate on a diagram of a female figure the hysterogenic zones—on the front, eleven in number, on the back six. It was an illustration that actually described myself, though in graphic form. I could then record the image of a human being's puzzling emotional life in a sketch with simplified clarity. Not until later did it occur to me that this was me, a human being, and that I, instead of regarding myself as so contradictory and chaotic, had been able to simplify myself to this—I hesitate to use the word—purity. This purity was what I strove to retain in my life ever since my experiences on the riverbank.*

Yet I still asked him questions that were irrelevant and almost hateful.

"Do you think I'm a machine and not a human being, sir?" I asked; at that time I was still addressing him in the formal manner.

"No," he defended himself, but he glanced away as if the words felt like an accusation.

"But you do believe," I persisted, "that by touching these points you will have me in your power?"

He did not reply.

★ ★ ★

His assistant Sigmund once asked her about her childhood and upbringing.

"Did you ever feel desire for your brother?" he asked.

"Of course," she replied.

He saw that she was smiling. *But,* she writes, *what stories won't a person seize upon now, long afterwards, after her life has ended and she's been put in a wooden box on wheels!* When she was fourteen years old, still a child, with childish thoughts and the lack of forbearance and forgiveness of a rabies-infected wolf toward life, her father once came back to see his wife. She wasn't home. *My mother hated him, and he hated her. I hated her too, but only until that moment when she, swallowed up by the embrace of the river, left me. Then I burst out sobbing, as if confronted with an amputated love.* Blanche's father spoke to her politely; he went out into the garden and picked three flowers, which he gave to her as if she were a stranger, an unknown and beautiful young woman.

He left; it was dusk. But she stopped him at the garden gate, took him by the shoulders, turned him around to face her, and gave him a long kiss, as if he were a man and she a woman. *I took pleasure in his kiss. I miss him terribly. And this young rascal asks me about my brother, about whether I feel desire for him!*

Certainly not. But three flowers! Yellow! She thought it was comical.

It may be possible to talk your way to the point where the inexplicable becomes visible, even from a wooden box on wheels.

But that doesn't mean you understand.

She says to Marie that she *hated Charcot from the very first moment, but later she no longer hated him; instead she loved him.*

In the end she loved him very much.

It's simpler that way. A love story in summary. It can start off like that, with loathing. Later everything changes. *You're the one I love and will always love, for an eternity of eternities.*

Blanche was eighteen when she was confined to Salpêtrière.

It was not the first time she was confined; since the age of seventeen she had been admitted and released from several institutions. Madhouses, she used to say. Most people took that word *madhouses* as an example of arrogance. I've been confined to five madhouses, she might say with a calmly lowered glance, *beautiful as an alpine violet,* with an ominously gentle undertone intimating that madness might explode at any moment. She was so beautiful, after all. The man she came to love, Jean Martin Charcot, was born in Paris on November 29, 1825; he was the son of a wagon-maker.

It's necessary to search between the images, not within them.

He had no particular memories from his childhood. What he recalled best was the summer he spent on the coast of the Channel, near the town of Saint-Malo. He had a clear memory of that summer. Otherwise blank, no memories. Her repetitions are insane. Love was not something she could explain, but she tried.

Madhouses, she used to say. Hospital is undoubtedly more accurate, or asylum.

No one has ever—either before Salpêtrière or afterwards—described her as insane. Yet she was in and out of the madhouse, and always that calm, sweet, menacing beauty. She would fall apart at regular intervals, be admitted, cured, released, and then fall apart again. How well I recognize that!

As mentioned: She detested Charcot from the very first moment. Later she no longer did.

*   *   *

She had recurrent incidents of a "hysterical nature."

The attacks would start off with a tonic and later a clonic phase. Then, after a brief interval, and extreme *opisthotonus*, with *arc-de-cercle*, occasionally with *vocalization*. Then she would become dangerous, although beautiful. No one had any idea what to do.

I think everyone had given up on her.

For a long time people hope to be able to entice someone back to what is normal. Later on they give up. So Blanche Wittman was sent to Salpêtrière. It was like an end station, or a trash dump. The lunatics' castle, the women's castle, the trash castle for those who were hopeless.

But she was only eighteen!

Blanche entered into an ancient tradition at Salpêtrière; with eight thousand inmates it had been the largest asylum in eighteenth-century Europe. And in a town with a population of only half a million! which meant that often three or four were forced to share a bed, and where the section for depraved young women, or rather children, in particular, at La Maison de Correction, played an important role. Imprisoned at La Correction were young girls who were classified as either *perverted or degenerate*. They had been confined at the request of their families, a request that was submitted to the king or the administration of the Hospice Général. The parents, or in many cases the neighbors, sent in an application stating that the depraved girls were a nuisance to the family, or the neighbors, or, in a broader sense, to the immediate area in which they lived, such as a neighborhood. And the children would then be transferred to La Correction in Salpêtrière.

And how quickly convulsive symptoms would appear!

The perverted and depraved children were separated from the prostitutes' quarters, La Commune, only by an open square. These young girls did not have to endure the procedures designated for the prostitutes, which entailed being branded on the right shoulder with a "V" or a "fleur de lis" (perhaps she hadn't found the image of the branding iron in Racine after all!). Nor did they have anything to do with the many women who were categorized as "political prisoners" at La Grande Force where, particularly in the mid-1700s, the so-called ecstatic *convulsionnaires* of Saint-Médard were legendary within the Salpêtrière tradition.

Blanche was led into an entire history! Into the sullied history of modernity!

They led her into the Castle the way cattle are led into a pen.

She did not attempt to resist, but one of the attendants kept a tight grip on her arm, and when it hurt so badly that she *cried out convulsively*—the expression is most likely not correct, like so much else in the Book of Questions—he put his arm around her waist and later reassuringly stroked her breast. *I don't remember how many of those so-called hospitals I visited, or was forced to enter. But my father, as a solution to a problem that he didn't know how to master, told those in charge that I was sick in my head, that I had uttered false accusations against anyone and everyone, including himself. And the innocent attendants who led me into Salpêtrière Hospital couldn't be blamed for regarding me as a lunatic who had to be soothed. Much had also been reported in the newspapers about those who were ill with dropsy, also called rabies, to whom Doctor Pasteur had drawn so much attention. Maybe the attendants were afraid that I might infect them. It was well known, for example, how the rabies-infected Russian peasants who were brought to Paris, and whom Doctor Pasteur was now studying, how, either out of fear or dread, these lunatics would gnaw on the iron bars and throw themselves against the stone walls to put an end to their unspeakable suffering. So wasn't it possible that I, this terrifying young creature by the name of Blanche Wittman, who was often struck by rabies-like spasms, might also be infected?*

And so they had reassuringly stroked her breast and cheerfully led her in through the portal, which was the entrance to the castle where she would now spend sixteen years of her young life.

That was on April 12, 1878.

She was there for three months before she saw for the first time the man who ruled the Castle, the mighty Doctor Charcot, who was both admired and feared. *And when our eyes met, and he leaned over his casebook to study what had been recorded about me, I instantly experienced a feeling of hatred, a feeling that he did not share, and that I would later reshape into love. I knew that he wished to direct my life, and I knew that he would not succeed. From that moment on he was irretrievably lost.*

She doesn't write much more about her arrival.

Charcot's silence was well known.

Whenever he examined a patient in front of the audience on a Friday—later also on Tuesdays—he would often sit and look at her, silent and thoughtful. Then he might ask a brief question in a low voice that was almost a whisper, then again fall silent. Occasionally a sudden friendly smile that would just as quickly vanish, as if he had been struck by an idea that was abruptly erased from his mind.

Blanche was so young. It's not clear whether in the beginning he even paid any attention to her.

Very beautiful, her eyes lowered. How could he possibly have known?

3.

In 1657 begging was outlawed in Paris. Beggars were arrested and taken to Salpêtrière, which in the eighteenth century was Europe's largest asylum with more than eight thousand patients and prisoners.

No one could distinguish between these two concepts: patient and prisoner. So they agreed on "patient."

There they were all gathered: the old, the indigent, the beggars, the prostitutes with venereal diseases, the paralyzed, the chronically ill, the spastics, the insane, and the children who were wards of the state. Also those who could not be labeled in this way but who were transformed into one of these categories. The lowest of all those who were admitted lived in the belly of the Castle, the innermost abdominal cavity that was called Les Loges des Folles: dungeon cells with dirt floors, reserved for the women suffering from dementia. There the weakest patients were soon killed off by the countless aggressive rats, who, in the dark, staged a battle for survival, a battle that most often won out over the aging female intruders.

That was the Castle's innermost space, the innermost cavity of its belly: as if the Castle were almost a human entity. Inside this human creature there was a terrifying secret, an innermost room, the unexplored black nightmare of the human being.

But for a hundred years the appointed rulers of the Castle showed little interest in this innermost cavity.

Later it was said that Doctor Charcot's predecessors had improved the conditions.

Who penetrated and sought out the belly's cavity?

Philippe Pinel, perhaps? Born in 1745, a friend of Benjamin Franklin, later a man of the Enlightenment with dreams of traveling to America. Instead, he ended up as a doctor at Salpêtrière, and he remained there until his death in 1826. During the French Revolution, encouraged by the ideas of the Enlightenment, he suggested that the women prisoners who were treated worst should be freed from their shackles. He was then asked: *Citizen Pinel, have you too gone mad? To want to free these female animals!* whereupon he replied that they had gone mad because of the stench, the lack of fresh air, the thousands of rats, the darkness in the cells, and the hopelessness. *And the revolutionaries said: Do as you like, Citizen Pinel!* Several hundred women were then released into the light. An outraged crowd, frightened by the appearance of the freed women, threw itself at Pinel. But he was rescued by a soldier by the name of Chevigne, whom he had previously released after ten years in chains.

Yes, Charcot told Blanche in reply to her question one night shortly before his tragic death in her arms, *Pinel was my mentor.*

And in between? Between 1826 and 1862?

Many others.

But Pinel was his mentor.

4.

Was it a relief to tell her story to Marie?

It has to be imagined as a tragedy shaped on a theater's gigantic stage, where the stage was everything, the actors numbering in the thousands, and down in the audience only a handful of spectators.

No, only one, Marie Skłodowska Curie! Resplendent in love's deadly blue light! Waiting!

One time Blanche was measured.

It was done by Paul Broca, professor of neurosurgery and a specialist in the human cranium. He was a student of Lombroso, whose studies of the human cranium, in particular the brains of women and criminals, in which he saw certain striking similarities, would prove especially fascinating to August Strindberg.

Blanche did not like Broca. She thought that he basically regarded her as a beautiful animal whose skull could be measured and weighed. But how brilliantly this young girl Blanche, this lace-maker! understood how to defend herself against such spiritual tyranny! She found a quote from Hippocrates, a criticism of the relevance of measuring the shape of the human head. *Who could have foreseen, if proceeding only from the shape of the human brain, that a goblet of wine could cause such degeneration of its function?*

Charcot *laughingly praised my quote from Hippocrates*, and used it in one of his lectures. *We are fumbling our way inside a thoroughly unknown continent with you by the hand!* he said, and then silently gave her a long, searching look.

Did he mean Blanche in particular?

Or Woman in general?

At the time he arrived, Salpêtrière was called potentially the world's greatest center for clinical neurological research.

The young Charcot encountered a chamber of horrors of disease, a chaos of unclassified afflictions, of cries, pleas, and prejudices. The chamber of horrors was populated, Charcot wrote as early as 1867, by the mentally retarded, by those who were mentally ill, by idiots, by epileptics and lunatics, *all of whom were perhaps simply human beings.*

The phrase is no doubt deliberately vague: *perhaps simply human beings.*

At the center of this horde of "human rats" was a group of 2,500 women, for whose ailments no one had an answer; their enigma was so impossible to solve that they were quite simply confined, as bewitched but not treatable.

Blanche writes repeatedly that Salpêtrière *housed those who were bewitched.*

Why did Charcot stay at the hospital?

It was here, he once said, that the future of reason began.

When he went to the hospital for the first time, on a chance visit, and saw all that filth, that terror, those paralyzed limbs, the shaking, the trembling, the bellowing and anguished pleas, and knew that the world lacked any knowledge of neuropathology, he said to himself: "*Faudrait y retourner et y rester.*"

It's necessary to return here, and to stay.

It's the same with love, writes Blanche in her childishly rounded handwriting, *you get stuck for life, no matter how much you may wish for freedom.*

Wish for freedom! Which was not something he ever did.

As for Charcot and the Communards.

The creation of a national center for neurological research, with Charcot in the lead, was a way to restore the national *gloire* after the defeat of 1870 and the bloodbath in connection with the Communard uprising. The big amphitheater that was built on the site, intended for Charcot's larger public lectures, and the enormous sums that were invested in his research and demonstrations, also had a national purpose. The Friday lectures, those that were depicted in the famous painting with Charcot and the powerless Blanche, were now moved to the larger public arena, *Leçons du Mardi à la Salpêtrière.*

It could be said that this was France's era, shaped in the form of a theater performance called *The Powerless Blanche.*

Charcot was not allowed to touch her; only during the performances would she permit it, when everyone else was present. But then he chose to let his assistants do so. One time he wept, but steeled himself, and afterwards they carried out a thoroughly successful performance.

How difficult to distinguish the artistry of solace and healing from that of seduction!

I love you, he said. But she had refused to answer, and so after that Tuesday performance he had once again returned to his home and his wife and his children, and she to her room, and he to his room, and they both lay in their beds in the dark, an eternity of eternities apart from each other, staring up at the ceiling, and neither had any idea what to do.

Year after year? Marie Skłodowska Curie asked.

Year after year.

5.

At first enmity.

They approached each other slowly, circling like two samurais, waiting for the deadly attack.

Torn and partly censored pages in The Black Book regarding jealousy.

Charcot often saw her walk across the courtyard, heading for the office of Gilles de la Tourette; he took note of the fact, perhaps still with indifference still, that it was there she was going. After only a year she had been assigned her own room in the hospital. That was exceptional. She was well dressed. She was like a tropical fish that had gone astray. He may have wondered what she was doing in Gilles de la Tourette's consulting room.

He felt a slight irritation, for professional reasons.

Gilles de la Tourette had a *thoroughly scientific dream,* which Charcot with a hint of derision was accustomed to calling "A thousand and one nights." A group of his patients was used for it. The idea was that in the Castle people told stories in order to survive. The stories were often about love. Although de la Tourette had expected other types of stories, harsher ones; but they had to do with love. He couldn't deal with these accounts.

Charcot was suspicious. *Love as a neurological fit with catatonic elements.* Was it possible to *induce neurological fits by telling stories,* for example about love? Or even a reasonable explanation for *how it all made sense?* What was de la Tourette actually working on? The experimental group finally dwindled to a dozen, including Bas, Glaiz, and Witt, as their names were abbreviated in the records; there were actually only three, no more.

Then Charcot took over everything. Including Blanche. Bas and Glaiz were merely abbreviations that did not chafe on his soul like grains of sand. But Witt, meaning Blanche Wittman, was another matter entirely.

First many thousands. Then a dozen. In the end only one. Actually only one who counted.

Now it was just Blanche.

Witt, as he wrote in the records.

In the records he froze his love.

Witt was a human being on the human periphery. At first he regarded me as an oyster, she told Marie one night. You drop lemon juice on an oyster to see whether it's alive and really a human being. He dropped lemon juice on me. Then he was seized with love. That was his punishment. The punishment of love is the harshest of all, especially if the beloved is transformed from an oyster into a human being.

She wasn't sure that Marie was listening. Marie would often lie on the floor next to the wooden box, on a mattress, with her eyes closed. Do you understand, Marie? she asked, speaking into the darkness. Do you understand the image of the oyster?

The image! She is trying to disguise herself! This was no doubt the reason why Marie remained silent.

It's also possible to imagine Blanche as the unknown jungle in the interior of which Charcot has gone astray. And during the last years of his life he tries desperately to find his way out.

The first examination: actually a conversation in which he with interest drops lemon juice on Blanche, to see whether she contracts.

"I've noticed," Charcot stated in a very low voice, "that you keep away from the other inmates."

"That's correct."

"As if you were superior to them, a rather more sublime human being; or, what should we say, that you're afflicted with a somewhat more sublime ailment? Is that how you see it?"

She looked him right in the eye and said:

"Professor Charcot, I know that you hold all the power over this institution. Don't make yourself less than you are by pointing that out. I know. You think that I'm arrogant, you want to diminish me until I achieve the desired humility. That's why you're asking. You wish to have greater power over me."

"That's not what I asked," he said after a long silence.

"But I answered your question," she quickly retorted.

The word medicine, Charcot later told her, and he now addressed her in the informal manner, *comes from Medea, the mother of witchcraft*. Does that mean you're a magician? she asked. No, he said, I'm a prisoner of reason, with my feet buried deep in the mud from which magic is composed.

Does that mean that you want to be free? she asked.

He remained silent for a long time, then replied. Yes, he said, I want to be set free, but will never be free. Even if I succeeded in freeing my feet from this mud, it would still cling to me forever.

Is that why? she asked. That's why, he replied.

He said that his method could not be explained rationally, and it was best to continue to seek whatever could not be explained. She recorded—and she must have misunderstood something—the words: *love like medicine is a speculative method, strictly based on facts.*

In The Black Book the description of a growing tension.

He went into his office, leaving the door open; Blanche hesitated for a moment and then followed him. He did not turn around, but he knew that she was there. Behind the big green jar in which he had preserved the Badrois relics stood a small bookcase holding brown folders; he took out one of them and sat down at the desk. Blanche closed the door. He voiced no objections. She sat down next to him. His handwriting was easy to read. He ran his index finger along the text as he slowly read aloud.

He had such a beautiful voice. And she later told him as much.

During these private conversations he told her about what he called "the mysteries of the past." He included "*the great saltatory epidemics*" from the Middle Ages among these mysteries, the dancing epidemics such as Saint Vitus, or what was called "*chorea germanorum.*" In the dossier he collected information about those of his patients who came from different geographic regions. Those who were suffering from *diabolic transactions that solely touched limited areas*—he read aloud in his beautiful, calm voice, and there was an odd tension in the room, in his voice and in the grotesque scientific findings he was recounting. *I remember in particular one time when he told me about the great Jansenist François de Paris, who died at the age of thirty-seven from self-imposed starvation. He became a saintly figure among those who, for religious reasons, assumed the holy mantle of starvation. And later those who were ill, poor, and starving would gather at his grave in a cemetery in Paris; by praying and touching his gravestone, they sought to ease their own suffering.*

Finally there was a great crowd of ragged and miserable souls who displayed violent convulsions, spasms, and ecstatic leaps high into the air, trying to invoke the saint and receive relief and mercy. In the end this was too much for public morality. Since these grotesque theatrical performances at the quiet cemetery had aroused so much attention, King Louis XV then decided to close the cemetery, imprison those convulsive supplicants, and take them—of course—to Salpêtrière Hospital!

This was in the year 1732. During the recounting of this story, Blanche had interrupted him and cried Sorcery! whereupon Charcot, with a strange smile and almost as if to himself, had said: Yes, it's sorcery, but the sorcery that is a thread in the fabric from which our lives are woven.

He then told her about the Dutch reformer Jansen, who died in 1638 and was regarded by some as a heretic, although in Paris strong and secret cells of Jansenists still existed.

He had known many of them, he said, as if in passing, or as a vague attempt to entice Blanche into an area that he was not certain she wanted to enter.

Sorcery!

Was it really only sorcery? she asks, as if she were gathering material for a speech in defense of her lover.

Charcot was a pioneer in the field of neurological diseases, with major contributions to questions regarding, for instance, neuropathic inflammations in the long nerve fibers of the leg, "rats under the skin," also called Charcot's disease, and multiple sclerosis. But Blanche's speech in his defense takes a detour. *He detested Englishmen because of the fox hunts. He found any form of cruelty to animals detestable, and this included, in his opinion, all hunting.*

I asked him why. He said that animals, because they don't need to do anything to deserve love, or at least because they are so innocent, ought to be given love that is in some way of religious proportions. He used the word "agápe."

She then asked: So what about me? He answered, almost indignant: Don't you understand anything!!!

His secretary for a year during the 1880s was a young Austrian by the name of Sigmund Freud, and to him Charcot recounted an incident that occurred before his discovery of multiple sclerosis.

By chance he had come into contact with a cleaning woman who suffered from a strange form of shaking, which made it awkward for her to do her work, and for that reason she was unemployed. Charcot gave her employment in his home, and at first he diagnosed her difficulty as "Chorea paralysis," which had already been described by Duchenne. But he soon found that her condition, which was gradually growing worse, pointed in a different and as yet unknown direction. He employed her as his cleaning woman until her death, in spite of his wife's objections. And by studying her he set off on the path that would later lead to the conclusive identification and diagnosis of multiple sclerosis. This was also confirmed when the servant woman died, since Charcot, who naturally had access to his cleaning woman's corpse, was immediately able to perform an autopsy and had his analysis confirmed.

In this manner, he bore with her increasing clumsiness all the way up until her death, which led him onto the right track and made her last years both tolerable and humane.

Yet this was done at the cost of a tremendous quantity of broken china.

In the Book of Questions, Blanche returns numerous times to Charcot's cleaning woman, the one who turned out to be suffering from multiple sclerosis and who destroyed such a large quantity of Charcot's china without being blamed.

Did he also regard Blanche as this sort of patient? For that matter, was it really natural, after her death, to cut up his beloved cleaning woman's body? Wasn't it fair then, she asks in several places, for her to assume the doctor's role and he the patient's, the observed, diagnosed, and inferior? Love and the battle for power can never be separated, after all, as she once said.

He glared at her, utterly furious, and angrily left the room.

How little she understood! after all these years of failed experiments! he later told her, as an explanation for his outburst.

She then merely said:

"Failed?"

6.

No precise explanations, or dates, as to when the conflicts give rise to love.

Suddenly a remark in the Book of Questions that reveals a changed situation.

On February 22, 1886, Charcot came to see her, sat down, and took her hand.

He sat very quietly, without moving or speaking.

"What do you want?" she asked after a moment's silence.

He then merely stroked her hand cautiously, and replied:

"Nothing on this earth, or in heaven, if it exists, have I ever desired as much as this hand. This skin. This bone. This skeleton. I know how they all look, all the parts. But why do I desire precisely this hand? Is that the secret, Blanche? Is this hand the secret?"

"The secret?" she asked.

"Yes," he replied. "I can't sleep, I can't think. I think I'm as possessed as those in my care. I don't understand it. May I sit here with you for a while?"

"Why?" she then asked.

"What a torment it is, I can think only of you."

"A torment?"

"Night and day."

Then she didn't know what to say, whether this torment he described was actually herself, or whether he was trying to say something else that perhaps should have pleased her. There was a lengthy silence in the room. He did and said nothing, merely held her hand, gently stroking it.

"What do you want?" she asked. "Do you want to know how it all makes sense?"

"Nothing fills me with so much confusion and anguish as this hand."

"What should I do?" she said.

"Just sit here."

"Is that all?"

"Just sit here."

Much later.

She said: "I'm not stupid, I know that you love me, but our love is theoretically impossible."

He then told her:

"Theory is fine, but it can't make reality disappear."

She also used a different wording, later in the Book of Questions: Theory is fine, but it doesn't annihilate reality. "La théorie, c'est bon, mais ça n'empêche pas d'exister."

He actually uses the same wording when he talks about his science, and his scientific objections to a hypothesis. Theoretically this is lunacy. But it exists!

He did love her. He thought she was so splendid.

7.

It's important to picture Blanche as a young girl, all of whose experiences were of negligible value.

Then she was surprised by a sudden, insane, and completely innocent love, which this older ruler of a deranged and terrifying female castle *placed at her feet like a prayer.* Or an offering? perhaps besmirched by all she had seen and feared, and written down. *Regarding pains in the ovaries, the so-called ovary symptoms, the following methods could be used. If the patients —at their own request—required treatment for these pains in the abdomen, it could be done by using pressure, squeezing, delivering hard blows, or, in certain cases, "blows of the sword," in that swords, by using the flat of the blade, were beat against the belly until the pains ceased. In medical history this was the common method of treatment for this type of pain, but Charcot had pointed out the importance of not turning the blade so that cuts and bleeding resulted in the abdomen. He referred, by the way, to his disciple Désiré-Magloire Bourneville, who in the book* Science et miracle *extensively discusses the long path of the miracle into modern science.* But how was she supposed to protect herself from what she saw! and how was she supposed to understand that this ruler of the Castle, Professor Charcot, was so helpless before her!

And what was it he sought from her?

Sought, and found.

They seem to have met in his office at Salpêtrière Hospital, always sitting chastely on either side of his desk, never intimate, conversing in low voices.

We have to imagine that those low voices possessed an intimacy, like skin against skin. Why else would they refrain from touching each other? Oh yes, the hand; it's true that one time he did hold her hand. But during the medical performances, when everyone was watching? No, he allowed only his assistants to touch the hysterogenic points. Never himself.

But here: distance, and the uttermost closeness.

What was it he sought from her? And how did he explain her role in the public experiments when she, like a machine, was forced into a somnambulant state, and later reawakened? What was the purpose?

Charcot once explained to her that he had dreamed of a situation when the human being, *the real human being,* could be freed from what surrounded or rather shaped him. He occasionally used the word "machine" as synonymous with "like an animal." Meaning with feelings that are purer than a human's.

Purity! How terrifying.

To Blanche he had explained that the idea, or ideas, which are formed during a person's lifetime and shape him in this manner could, in the hysterical state, be screened off from that person. A glass bell is placed, metaphorically speaking, over the human being, *over the human being if such a thing really exists.* Over his upbringing, his skills, both social and acquired; the whole human network of rules would be isolated from him, and only the original human being would remain. Meaning his *ego.*

And he added: *Only then could we see before us the human being in certain respects like a machine, as once dreamed by La Mettrie.*

She asked: The points that you indicate on my body, the points where you press, or where you order your white-garbed slaves to press, and where the catatonic attacks are evoked, are they the points that reach inside to *my true self*—and which for the first time summon that ego in all its simple, perhaps terrifying, and yet obvious clarity?

In certain respects, he replied.

Am I then, by virtue of being a machine, freed from the filth of life?

Perhaps, he replied. But in some senses you are closer to your human self than you have ever been before.

As if I were an animal? she asked.

In certain respects, he repeated, in a low voice, and with love.

8.

One time in the spring of 1888 they had a dispute.

Blanche does not write about what it entailed, but it resulted in her rushing out of his office "shrieking," and after that Charcot, in anger, turned over her treatments to his colleague Jules Janet. By then Blanche had acquired a reputation for her dramatic talent to create characters comparable to that of Sarah Bernhardt. The young Janet, in order to make an impression on his peers, had summoned an audience consisting of jurists, researchers, and specialists in medical jurisprudence in order, with Blanche's help, to solve or at any rate to elucidate the question of to what extent *a woman in a somnambulant state could commit a crime.*

Blanche was magnificent.

Obediently and with theatrical ferocity she carried out the most bloodthirsty tasks, such as killing with a knife, murdering with a gun, and poisoning. When the invited notables left the scene it was, metaphorically speaking, covered with corpses and body parts, and the performance had clearly confirmed that the somnambulant hysteric was fully capable of committing criminal acts.

Several of Janet's students stayed behind, however, and one of them, on behalf of his fellow students, told Blanche, who was still in a somnambulant state, to undress and take a bath. Blanche, in a furious outburst, then screamed that the student's suggestion was vile, and she chased the terrified youth out the door.

Blanche's furious outburst lasted for such a long time that Charcot was summoned, and Blanche, with a stubborn demeanor and a composure that to Charcot felt almost deadly, ominously demanded an explanation for why he had been unfaithful. Charcot didn't understand, but she kept repeating the word "unfaithful," and by that she clearly meant that he had turned her over to the care of another researcher.

This was a vile and unfaithful act, and she had been demeaned. He then asked what the difference could be, since even with him she had performed in public. She then tried to strike him.

This led to a long scene between them. Gradually their voices grew lower. Those who were listening out in the corridor had the impression that in the end both fell silent.

Then they left the room; it was apparent that both of them had wept.

In the Book of Questions, indications of jealousy, or a struggle for power.

Blanche had been under the care of Jules Janet before.

As late as January 1886 she was taken to the hospital ward of Hôtel-Dieu at Salpêtrière—for a period when Charcot was ill—and hypnotized there. She was then subjected to "mesmeric passage," but also taken further to a vague state that was assumed to be Gurney's deep state. Attempts were made to complement this with Azam's variant of total somnambulism, later with a combination of Azam and Sollier. But upon awakening twenty-four hours later, Blanche remained in an inexplicably dissociated condition, which in her file was recorded as Blanche 1 and Blanche 2.

During Blanche 1 she was very pliable and spastic, almost loving. During Blanche 2 she was very quiet and distressed, and she pleaded *to go back to Charcot.*

9.

One of the few accounts that exist about Blanche Wittman after Charcot's death is found in A. Baudoin's "Quelques souvenirs de la Salpêtrière," in *Paris Médicales* 26: 517-520.

He makes contact with her by way of acquaintances of Marie Curie, and after several months—by then she has been severely amputated with only her left leg still to be cut—he dares ask the crucial question.

It should be added that Marie is not present during this conversation.

He asks her whether she was conscious of the degree of deception behind the somnambulant and hypnotic states. Whether the fits and the catatonic states were simulated. She replies in an ice-cold manner and without raising her voice:

"Simulated? Do you think it would have been easy to deceive Professor Charcot? Oh yes, there were plenty of women who tried to deceive him. Then he would merely give them a look and say: 'Be still!'"

Six months later Baudoin read in a newspaper that she was dead. So the conversation must have taken place sometime in 1912. This is the only documented interview with Blanche that exists after Charcot's death, the only text that can complement the Book of Questions.

Don't give up.

I'm still hoping that Blanche had a secret or covert plan in her Book of Questions that would make sense of it all. The hysterical fits must have begun sometime after her seventeenth birthday. The first diagnoses indicate epilepsy, but it quickly becomes clear that things aren't that "simple." And those pictures of her, meaning the painting and the one photograph.

But behind the pictures another image.

Someone who is knitting; someone who, wrapped up in herself, broods over a life that is slowly ebbing away; someone who is crocheting a glove, it could be during the Second World War, that's when it must be, she is crocheting a glove with the trigger finger free, no doubt it's something that will be sent to the Finnish soldiers during Finland's Winter War.

What is her name? She is crocheting a glove. At night inexplicable sobs that frighten the child.

One evening Charcot complained to Blanche Wittman, saying that Salpêtrière could still never compete with Lourdes in matters of faith.

Blanche asked him what he actually meant by the odd phrase "matters of faith." And he then evasively began talking about François de Paris and his gravesite, and about how his own father had brought him up as a Jansenist.

Blanche recounted this to Marie Curie. It prompted Marie's interest in the problem of Lourdes, *and changed her rigid attitude toward nuclear physics.* What a ridiculous claim, lacking in any historical basis.

Suddenly an astonishing remark in the Book of Questions, in a different tone:

And Charcot said: A miracle-worker can say to his patient: Stand up on your legs and walk! Why shouldn't we then play along with this game, if it's to the patient's benefit? But I say to all of you: Don't ever do such a thing, with certain isolated exceptions, on those occasions when you are completely certain about your diagnosis. Otherwise no. I say to all of you: Never prophesy unless you know.

An enlightened man with one foot in occultism. The horror that these enlightened men feel for the unknown! Those prejudices and safeguards! *Never prophesy unless you know.*

But then!

He seemed to regard love as an illness that could be induced.

The first time he touched her it was not Blanche but Charcot who grew utterly still. That was on March 22, 1878. He had seen her a month earlier when she was admitted to Salpêtrière Hospital and was given her diagnosis by his friend, Doctor Jules Janet. Now he saw her for the second time.

Charcot had perused her file for a long time without raising his eyes; then he glanced up and looked at her.

"Blanche," he said, "it says in the file that you are nearsighted. Is that true?"

She was sitting on a chair in front of him; she met his glance and smiled. Then he asked if he might hold her hand, to determine, as he said, whether the spasms had damaged the long nerve fibers. She gave him her hand.

Then it took until August 16, 1893, before he seized possession of her. That was how long it took.

She didn't answer his question about being nearsighted, and he didn't ask about anything else. But from that moment, which in reality lasted for nearly two hours, from that moment he loved her, and he didn't know it.

And from that moment she would change his life.

By the way, it was true. She was nearsighted.

10.

Nevertheless. They are approaching each other. They will soon begin.

There is only one detailed report in which it specifically says that Charcot uses Blanche Wittman as a subject for his experiments. Countless others describe experiments in which the woman is anonymous.

But in this case it says "Witt."

According to the introduction of the report, Charcot had a conversation with Blanche before the public treatment. He then showed her the ovary compressor, *which he might decide to use*. It was made of leather with metal screws affixed to it. It was placed over the woman's abdomen and buckled tight with leather straps fastened around her back. Both screws had protective leather padding. When the screws were slowly tightened, the leather padding would squeeze together the woman's uterus. The ovary compressor was applied to her bare stomach and then pressed down toward the hysteric center, to stop the attacks.

In this manner the unfortunate and desolate woman was supposed to achieve a sense of calm, with the help of this invention which has entered medical history under the name of ovary compressor.

The ovary compressor, he told her, is not a miraculous remedy; it can be used only to stop an attack. And there is so much misunderstanding concerning this purely mechanical remedy. I don't intend to use it today. He then grew more and more furious. *This ovary fixation! As if everything evil comes from the ovaries or uterus! And could be cut away!*

At first he spoke in a low and persuasive voice, then became overtly agitated; but why did he speak to her? And, incidentally, someone must have recorded their conversation; a third person must have been in the room. In the Book of Questions the same conversation is recounted, but in a more personal way, as if a third, mysterious, and in the records anonymous person never existed. There is something childlike about his eyes, she writes, *when he on these occasions allowed himself or condescended to speak with me.* A child's eyes, as if he were afraid, or was appealing to her, or wanted to make her understand, or felt guilty.

Guilty? guilty!!! Could that be why he spoke to her?

The worst misunderstandings come from America, he told her, *they're mad about using the knife over there, they surgically remove the uterus, cut off the labia; they remove the clitoris. They think that a woman's ovaries can wander around inside the body, that the removal of the ovaries will cure everything from epileptic seizures to hystero-epilepsy. A certain Doctor Spitzka at the American Neurological Foundation has hinted that I'm insane because I seek non-surgical ways to health, but I would never think of cutting you, Blanche. You know me. I never use animals for experiments, I love animals, I would never use a woman like an animal!*

She then interrupted him and said *when I was fifteen I lost my mother, whom I loved very much, in an accident at a river crossing, and the pain I then felt has been encapsulated inside of me and now provokes these convulsive fits.* For a moment he stared at her in astonishment, as if he didn't understand the connection, but after that, using a blunt ink pen, he began marking the pressure points on her body.

He explained that by pressing on these points he would provoke the states in her that in certain respects would imitate *or restore* the catatonic states that were curative. He talked as he marked the points, talked in an increasingly agitated manner. *People have accused me of summoning forth in this hospital an illness that doesn't exist in reality! They say that this illness exists only in my own mind! But it does exist! I implore you, take a look at the world outside Salpêtrière, at those who have never had any contact with me or this hospital! Take a look at those miserable souls, women and men! I tell you, these hysterical diseases can also be found in men!*

In Germany they mocked him and wrote that these hysterical illnesses *in that case exist only in French men, who are more effeminate!* He replied that all these illnesses could also be found among the strongest of men! among miners and construction workers! *No, I would never dream of summoning forth an affliction that does not exist; no, I'm not that sort of person. I am a photographer of humanity, I describe what I see.*

I am a camera, and people are now accusing this camera of lying.

He actually says that: "*I am a camera.*" But not in the 1930s of German decadence, as in Isherwood, but at Salpêtrière!

Europe! that fantastic Europe!

*   *   *

It was an indignant monologue. He seemed to be in despair. Blanche, for the most part, sat in silence.

The audience was waiting, increasingly impatient. He didn't want to go out to them.

And in me, what do you see? she asked. I see you, he said after a long silence. I am the first to see you, and that's why we will now go out to this demonstration. I asked what you see, she said. If only I knew, he replied after a long silence. If only I knew. But you'll go with me, won't you? he asked, almost in a whisper, like a child.

And then they went together to the lecture and demonstration, which Charcot held on February 7, 1888, at three o'clock in the afternoon.

11.

She had learned that it was not a matter of seeking out the way things were but instead the way things ought to be.

That was a person's own responsibility.

Yet you had to pretend to play along. Then, in the end, you would become enveloped in the way things ought to be. "The way things ought to be" was itself the solution. Then it was gentle and soft and unresisting. Then it was possible to endure.

There was always a moment that was *oppressive* at the start of each demonstration, before she won over the spectators, that hostile jungle, those wild animals who were looking at her. Then the wild animals would disappear and she entered into the way things ought to be, *simply set off on the journey through the foliage! and move butterfly-like! no, flutter toward him! like that time in May when we met and then urgently touched each other, and yet didn't! and yet didn't!*

The time was 3:01 p.m. and she set off on the journey.

She knew that soon, through the trees, she would be able to discern the water. Perhaps it was a river, or a shore, perhaps a sea, no it was a river. She had to move cautiously between the trees, through the foliage, so as to prolong the process. It should open up slowly, almost breathlessly. She had to walk lightly and weight-lessly, almost floating, knowing that she was a butterfly, *isn't Blanche the name of a type of butterfly?* making her way through the foliage slowly and aimlessly, exactly the way butterflies in flight move, between the branches and leaves. And then more and more of the water would become visible.

And it was a river.

When she entered the Auditorium and saw the audience, then it was good to know that she would soon be flying through the foliage. Perhaps Charcot knew this too. Lately he had start-ed making his introductions shorter; no doubt he knew that she would close her eyes, and then things would be the way they *ought to be.*

It was important to enter into what was *breathless.* The way it ought to be.

Charcot had such a calm and beautiful voice; she had always thought as much. The fact that he talked didn't disturb her. *This patient who will be used for the demonstration is not a machine, I want to tell you that right from the start, and so the experiment may fail. The human being is less predictable than a machine, that's what makes us human. Experiments on animals in the auditorium are also different from experiments in the laboratory under controlled conditions. The same holds true in this case. This patient, who suffers greatly from hysteric attacks and convulsions has a hysterogenic point on her back, another under her left breast, a third on her left leg. And the final phase in today's treatment, which is viewed as part of the healing process, may thus result in an extreme opisthotonus, meaning a classic arc-de-cercle. My assistant will first touch the point on her back.*

She knew what would happen, and she was prepared for what would happen.

It was a ceremony that was difficult in the beginning, but then it became the way it ought to be. It took several minutes;

the moment when she stepped through the door was the worst, when the murmuring stopped and everyone's eyes turned toward her, the person whom they were all now talking about, the famous one! the medium! The woman who was called Blanche and who possessed such an extraordinarily poignant beauty. The queen of the hysterics! And who, suddenly, could be transformed before their very eyes into a woman with many faces, and become Blanche 2 and Blanche 3 and Blanche 12; the one who confirmed their secret suspicions that not only this woman but all women had many faces. And what was terrifying, what everyone suspected, was the idea that something existed beyond their control! utterly beyond control! that what was terrifying might now be tamed, or be made scientifically comprehensible.

He had such a beautiful voice.

The assistant then touched the hysterogenic point, though not the one on her back as Charcot had said, but the one under her left breast. It didn't matter.

She was ready, she had set off.

She would go through the forest that consisted of deciduous trees, she would once again be fifteen years old, it would be that decisive spring and summer. Always in the afternoon.

Deciduous trees.

I'm going now, now I'm going, soon the forest will open, and she would make her way to the riverbank, and there the boy would be waiting for her, and he would say, when he saw her emerging from the trees, that *she was a butterfly that had escaped from heaven*, because that was the most splendid thing a person could say. That's why he would say it.

She closed her eyes and slipped into her tonic phase and walked through the forest.

Yet again she had managed to flee. The forest. The water. She saw him through the trees, and stopped; it was the way it ought to be. It was utterly right. Bare-legged, he stood a few meters out, having rolled up his pants to the knees, having turned his back to her, he was looking down at the flowing stream. She came out of the forest on the shore. The shore was devoid of people. They were alone, it was the way it ought to be. It was 3:12 in the afternoon, Blanche 2 found herself in an experimental setting at Salpêtrière Hospital and was called Witt, yet she was a butterfly that had escaped from heaven; now it was 3:17, and she called to the boy, who turned around and smiled.

She had come at just the right moment. He was a boy who was almost a man and he smiled at her. 3:18.

The first time they met in town, she thought he was very endearing, and he had laughed so splendidly and said that he would write a poem for her, and one day in the spring he had brought the poem. Written on a scrap of paper, on the back of a shopping list he was supposed to take along to the grocery store, and it started off so splendidly. She would always remember the first verse:

You are like a butterfly that has escaped from heaven,
you grew bored up there,
and want to play with me. You flutter toward me
and are a bit frightened.
Though I know who you are. God's butterfly,
in disguise.

God's butterfly, in disguise. That was Blanche. That was something a person could live on for a lifetime, she thought much later.

Since then she had heard him say that many times, that she was a runaway butterfly from heaven. And that she was in disguise. The word disguise was so splendid. It meant that she could hide within herself. Since then they had started meeting down by the shore. He used to arrive first, and he would wait for her. It was so grand and pure, but above all pure. That's why she had started going back to him whenever the wild animals gathered at Salpêtrière and looked at her before they threw themselves upon her with their eyes. That was now.

Foliage. Water. 3:22 p.m.

She walked through the foliage and stepped out onto the shore and knew that she was a butterfly, in disguise. She had told the boy, who would soon be grown up, like her, that he should barely touch her because you had to be careful with a butterfly. That's why it had been so splendid and pure. It was important for it to be pure. Now she had walked through the forest and foliage and over to the riverbank and called to him. He turned around and came toward her, as she stood on the shore.

3:24. She sat down on the grass near the riverbank.

He was suntanned and she knew that his skin was soft and that she could depend on him, which was the prerequisite. *This patient, only a minute ago, as you could observe, was completely rigid; the rigidity occurred very quickly, which is not common, and you must not draw hasty conclusions since each patient has individual patterns— thus, the fact that a final phase occurs that resembles delirium is also uncommon, but certainly possible. The traditional patterns are not the ones that are common; rather, they are uncommon, and thus must* and the boy stood for a moment in front of her, without moving, and looked at her. His torso was bare, his skin had a deep tan, and she knew that he was fifteen years old, just as she was, but to herself she called him a boy.

It was the same thing every time. 3:26.

She walked through the foliage and saw the water, then she reached the riverbank and he was standing out in the water; he turned around, smiled, and came toward her.

They lay down next to each other in the grass.

Very carefully he unbuttoned her blouse, pulled it aside and placed it next to her. He touched her breast with the back of his hand. The same thing held true every time they met; he was allowed to caress her, she was allowed to caress him, that was all.

And that was also everything, she knew, the highest and the purest, nothing could be higher. It would always be afternoon, with slanting sunlight. The sun would come through the foliage, not blazing but filled with shadows and it would wrap around them there on the riverbank. He had no name. Touch me, she says, but no more. You're allowed to do everything, but this is enough.

3:38. Now is when it happens. What has to happen.

Cautiously. The boy's hand glides across her breast and she moves her hand over his back and it is beautiful. When the sun sets, the sound of the water lapping against the rocks of the shore is audible. It's as if a glass bell were arched above them, and he says you can do what you like. Then she does, she uses her hand to caress wherever she wants to caress, is it good? she says. Yes, he says, one day we'll do everything, won't we?

She doesn't answer. She has walked through the forest and through the foliage, unhesitating as a butterfly, having escaped but conscious of her goal. She is utterly safe and she senses a warmth down below, and there is no fear whatsoever in that warmth. We do what we want, and one day, she says, one day we'll do everything. She touches him, and now he is lying completely naked beside her, and he curls up as if in spasm and then lies still and looks straight up into the sky. That's where you escaped from, he says, what do you want me to do? You should do, she says, whatever should be done with a butterfly that has escaped from heaven, has been a little bored, and wants to play with you.

And is a little frightened, he says. But I see who you are. One of God's butterflies, in disguise.

Yes, she says. Cautiously. Cautiously.

It's almost dusk, and it's splendid, and she doesn't ever want to wake up, *let us once again exert pressure on a few of the hysterogenic points. We can wait with the ovary compressor. As all of you can see, my assistant exerts a firm but not painful amount of pressure on the points in the ovary region. Notice the expression of pain that suddenly, and without any physiological cause, appears. Patients may often utter exclamations such as* **Mamma, I'm scared!** *Notice the emotional nature of the outburst, see here an* **arc***; if we allow this to continue, injury may occur; notice now the sudden calm, almost resolve, the static contracting stage is now dissipating.*

The sun was gone; dusk. What a strange darkness. She could no longer see the shore across the river. The boy was gone, and dusk fell swiftly, darkness flowed in from the east, and it was slightly chilly.

5:03 p.m. She had to find the path back through the forest.

How did that verse he had written go, the one about the butterfly in flight? Things had to return to normal, what was it he wrote in his poem? The path through the forest: so easy to find the riverbank, and so difficult to return! Like a butterfly that has escaped from heaven. Wants to play. Is frightened? She was enveloped by the boy at the riverbank. Now she will soon be back in the terrifying forest.

No foliage, only jungle.

All the wild animals were looking at her, in silence. The boy had seen who she was, and told her. God's butterfly, in disguise.

Now it was Marie's turn.

It required a superhuman effort, she had to make sense of it all. She knew that she would be able to do it.

VII

The Song of the Wild Animals

1.

THERE ARE TREES OUTSIDE THE WINDOWS OF MARIE'S APARTment in Paris.

Blanche was sleeping less and less; she was in pain. The pain would often come just before dawn, but then she could see out the window, could see the light arriving, the tree trunks becoming visible, then the shadows that perhaps were leaves, then the actual leaves. It was like the path to the riverbank. When she had almost arrived, it was best, as in the past. The young boy would be standing in the water, his torso bare and deep tan, he would turn to face her, and then she would see that his face was Charcot's, and she had known this all along.

When she wrote down certain conclusions about this, she did so in clear block letters. Then the words were almost rectangular, there was no hesitation, as if she had settled something, but previously hadn't dared. Or like a cry for help. *How do we survive love? How are we supposed to live without love?* That was something she ought to tell Marie. She was almost convinced of that, but first she had to understand it herself.

I'll never leave your side. The feeling that a *person without bene-*

factors has always lived under a glass bell, desperately scratching fingernails against glass, unable to get out. And then suddenly someone was there.

And someone whispered *I'll never leave your side.*

Marie asked Blanche why she sometimes thought that she had killed Charcot. Because, she replied, when I followed him out from the trees. And met him at the riverbank. And when he understood that I loved him. Then he didn't have the strength to fight against the darkness. If you share your darkness with the man you love, sometimes a light appears that is so strong that it kills.

You ought to know, Marie! After all, you've seen that deadly blue light!

Is that really love? asked Marie.

2.

Twice Blanche writes in the Book of Questions about *the turning point.* By the second time, she understands.

Then her introductory question is **When did I receive the explanation for Marie's breakdown?** (the first time the word used was the ambivalent "dilemma"). It has to do with the theft of the L'Arcouest letter. Blanche no doubt finally understood the consequences.

Incidentally, the same description of that terrible night.

Marie came rushing into my room, threw herself to her knees next to my wooden box; her face was deathly pale and her hair in disarray. She expressed the greatest despair and resignation with that stern and closed look on her face that made me wish she would cry, even though she said she couldn't. A break-in had occurred at the love nest that Marie and Paul shared; someone had stolen the letters that Marie had written to Paul. Among them, and this was the worst, was the long letter that she had written from L'Arcouest in August 1910. I asked her why that particular letter signified such great danger; she replied: it

should never have been written. Then why did you write it? I asked. It
was love, she replied.

Everybody seemed to know, but it had not been made public.
Now it was made public.

On November 3, 1911, the Solvay Conference came to an
end. Marie and Paul had both attended. Marie had become
embroiled in a heated argument with Rutherford about the
nature of decay produced by beta radiation. Einstein wrote in a
letter to Heinrich Zangger that during the conference he had
spent a great deal of time with Marie and Paul; "they are truly
delightful people; Madame Curie even promised to come and
visit me with her daughters." Einstein also describes his great
appreciation of Marie's "passion and sparkling intelligence." But
on the day after the conference ended, on November 4, 1911,
Marie's life fell apart, and from then on she was never again able
to devote herself to her research.

It is the newspaper *Le Journal* that declares, on the front page
as its main news story, that Marie Skłodowska Curie has
destroyed a man's marriage. There is a picture of her. The headline reads: "A Love Story: Madame Curie and Professor Langevin."
The article starts off with the words: "*The heat of radium, with its
mysterious blue glow, has now lit a fire in the heart of one of the scientists
who studies its activity with such intensity, while the same scientist's wife
and children weep in resignation.*"

The mysterious blue glow. Marie, Marie, now it's starting.

If a person is very high up, the fall is deep and hard.

And it was a fall, everyone seemed to agree about that. Even
Marie, who had fallen into the burning crater and could suddenly feel the pain. Which was unfair! unfair! All she had done
was love him!

But there were the children, after all. What the children would have to endure! The girls, the school, what she couldn't control, and what would befall the children!

The children!

Not a single newspaper could refrain from foaming with fury. *Le Petit Journal* said that it was necessary to take up once again the Dreyfus debate they had previously lost: Marie was most certainly a Jewess, and the connection, no matter how remote, was obvious. It was a Jew and a foreigner who now threatened *the French family* from within. Once again the same thing! like in the army! like in politics!

An interview was prominently published with Jeanne Langevin, dissolved in tears, *who was modest and shunned publicity*, but who had her mother give a detailed analysis of the home-wrecker Marie Skłodowska Curie, who was Polish, unfeminine, and cared only for books, her laboratory, and fame.

The respectable newspapers unanimously distanced themselves from Marie. This was on November 6. On November 7, 1911, when the scandal was at its peak, the Reuters news bureau sent out a wire reporting that Marie Curie had been awarded the 1911 Nobel Prize in Chemistry.

It was the first time anyone had ever been awarded two Nobel Prizes. Not a word about the award in the French press. What shame! What shame that an immoral woman had destroyed a French family, and also what shame for France that a "French" researcher, under these odious circumstances, should be awarded a Nobel Prize!

And so it was best not to mention it.

I have to flee, she told Blanche on that night. I have to disappear with my children. They've torn the clothes from my body, I stand naked before everyone, what shame!

"I know how you feel," replied Blanche.

"How can you know?"

"Marie," Blanche then said, "you find yourself in a situation that I'm quite familiar with. The wild animals are looking at you. Their rapacious eyes tell you that they want to attack soon, and tear you apart. But you're wrong. They don't want to kill you. Their desire is lecherous, not deadly. They're looking at your body because they covet it."

But she didn't understand, and Blanche couldn't explain. Just imagine, she said, that you're walking through the forest, and soon a glade will open up, and you see.

"Then what?" asked Marie. "What do I see?"

"The water. A river. There stands the one you love, and then you're no longer alone, and he will never leave your side."

Except that he would.

Paul Langevin's friends were summoned by the police prefect Louis Lepine. It was November 9, 1911, two days after the announcement of the Nobel Prize awarded to Marie Curie.

His friends were Jean Perrin and Émile Borel.

The police prefect had an offer to make. If Paul Langevin would unconditionally relinquish custody of the children and grant his wife support of one thousand (1,000) francs per month, a scandal could be avoided and the letters, in particular Marie's long letter, which would *obliterate her chances for conducting research within her scientific field,* would remain unpublished.

They returned from the meeting with police prefect Lepine and presented the proposal to Marie and Paul. Marie stated that it would have to be Paul's decision. And she would give him a free hand. Paul then stated that the proposal was unacceptable.

That meant war.

In a practical sense it also meant an end to Marie's scientific career. Shortly afterwards, and as a consequence of this decision, *L'Œuvre* published a nine-page supplement that contained all of Marie's love letters to Paul and, in extenso, the long letter she had written to Paul in August 1919 from L'Arcouest. That was the letter with the cold instructions as to how he could win his freedom, and the furious outbursts of hatred against his wife; it was the letter that should never have been written, but above all should never have been published. And the whole thing was quoted. "*With scientific sophistication she describes various ingenious methods for tormenting the poor wife so that she will become desperate and force a rupture.*" Everything, everything was dragged out.

It was all so ugly; oh, Marie, how ugly it all was.

And then everything, everything, came out.

3.

Later Marie turned up in Sceaux.

The girls had come home from school. Someone had shown her daughter Irène a newspaper story about her mother. A couple of well-meaning friends had read aloud part of it and explained that the newspapers were writing this because her mother was a whore. Then the girl didn't want to hear any more but raced off for home. No one was home except Blanche.

Irène crept into Blanche's bed, at the foot, saying she was tired and wanted to go to asleep. But she couldn't sleep because she was shaking all over; then she helped Blanche into her mobile wooden box and pushed her around and around the room as she "told her everything."

The girl had told her everything, meaning she screamed uncontrollably.

Blanche asked her to stop pushing her around and around, but she didn't seem to understand and merely continued. Then Marie came home, yanked away her daughter, who kept on screaming loudly, as if in sorrow or despair, and hastily got her dressed. On this occasion Blanche tried on her own to pull herself out of the wooden box to prevent Marie from fleeing, but she fell and rolled around on the floor.

That was the beginning of the journey to the little French town of Sceaux.

Suddenly Blanche found herself alone in the apartment.

She jotted down certain observations in the Book of Questions, this time in her hard-to-read handwriting, instead of printing.

With some difficulty she managed to move across the floor *without the aid of my transport box,* successfully made it to the kitchen that evening and prepared a light meal, but above all she says that she was worried about Marie and her two children.

It was the children, she writes over and over. No comments about Paul, except for an unbalanced tirade.

She looks out the window, discovers *the group of people who were watching the alleged whore's residence. This group slowly became a crowd, which reminded me of those days at Salpêtrière when the audience seemed to look at me as if the crowd were a rapacious and bloodthirsty wild animal. But after Marie fled and after she returned, when I presented this almost poetic metaphor to Marie, as a form of consolation, she found in it little solace, and kept repeating that the innocent children had suffered the brunt of it, and that I, Blanche, in spite of everything, had suffered my degradation alone, had not been responsible for any children. I had nothing to say in reply.*

Marie fled to Sceaux with her children. A week later they returned to Paris, and to Blanche. What had happened?

Fragmented comments in the Book of Questions.

It's necessary to reconstruct.

4.

The fall so great, the shame so deep, the reputation of a long life obliterated, and she was absolutely, utterly helpless.

Why does it have to be like this? she thought.

She felt shame but at the same time it was unfair, because did she have to be ashamed of her love? Sceaux was a dead town, she thought, as if it were on Greenland. Perhaps like Nome, no not Nome! that was something quite different and without pain! Nome should be the word for a pleasure and a passion that was hidden. Everything all around obliterated! and no history! and no future! No, somewhere else.

Like a forest in Poland, a cabin in a glade in a Polish forest.

In Sceaux she still had the house in which Pierre's father had lived.

It was almost always empty: now in November an atmosphere of sorrow hovered over the empty rooms, a moldy chill, with turn-of-the-century furnishings, now abandoned, a wooden floor that had once been well-scrubbed, white tulle curtains *with moth holes like a reputation that had been eaten away,* as she suddenly thought in an almost poetic image. She arrived in the evening, late, with her girls: a terrible journey, Marie white in the face and the girls mute.

And what should they have said?

She put the girls to bed and begged them to fall calmly asleep, and they lovingly complied with their mother's urgent entreaty. Then she went to visit the grave.

She went straight to the cemetery.

5.

It was late at night, the streets were deserted, and she was almost certain that the flood of rumors had not yet reached little Sceaux.

Here she would be able to rest.

There must be some way out, even for someone who was so alone; *is there no one who will take pity on the woman! Can't you see! Up toward the house through the snow?* If a person took the dizzying step into the great loneliness, in the end there had to be mercy for her too.

To think the shame could be so great, when she thought that she had merely been in love.

Why did it all have to be so ugly!

As if at first love was dizzying and warm and almost burning, but then what had been magma and hot turned black and grotesque and hardened and was transformed into shameful lava. And the children. How could she explain it to them? Wasn't there some little town in Poland where she could hide? And then there was the hatred. She felt such an intense hatred that she couldn't breathe. Not their hatred. Her own! She was so ugly with hatred! Ugly!

It wasn't fair.

It had happened so fast, she had been so happy, and so imprudently in love, so utterly unscientifically in love. But to think that she had made it so easy for them!

She started thinking about them the way Blanche did.

As wild animals.

The cemetery was pitch-dark, but she knew the way.

This was where Pierre had been buried five years earlier, this was where Pierre's father had been buried only a year and a half ago. The darkness was chilly and there was a light rain; she searched for a while, it was difficult, the gravel paths were muddy, no grass.

Then she found the grave.

The headstone had been put up quite recently. Pierre's name was on it, and his father's. She knelt down without thinking, felt the ice-cold mud against her knees. It was humiliating; she wanted to stand up but didn't. It was dark, after all, no one could see her in this absurd situation. The absurdity of it all would be her punishment. She was undoubtedly to blame. Pointless to try to evade blame.

The grave was narrow; she suddenly realized with almost shocked sorrow that the coffins had been placed on top of each other, that Pierre's coffin was underneath, that his father's had been placed on top of him, and that she herself, if she would be allowed to rest here, *if she would be allowed to rest here!* would not have the place closest to Pierre Curie. It was almost obscene, she felt nausea rising inside her, it was preposterous, it couldn't be true.

She had been shut off from Pierre as well.

It was not the fault of her father-in-law. She had liked him. But now she realized that she, even here, had been shut out. He died in March 1910, before everything broke loose; now he was placed like a roof over her beloved Pierre.

Death was punishing her; even death regarded her as a sinner.

She felt sick. She tried with all her might to control the nausea but failed; she threw up, turning her head so the vomit would fall to the side and not on Pierre's grave. It was mostly yellow phlegm; she hadn't been able to eat anything the past twenty-four hours. She tried to decipher the text on the gravestone, but it was nearly impossible in the dark. This was where she might be allowed to rest. What would it say? Marie the whore, despised by the French people, a disgrace to her children. It was here that it would all come to an end, at the bottom Pierre's coffin and above it his father's, the real Curies, and on top of them the coffin of the Polish woman. But not even in the closeness of the final embrace. What was it that Blanche had once said about love? It was a statement that would explain everything. Not about the way things were, but about the way they ought to be.

Oh yes, she remembered now. *I'll never leave your side.*

And here she was on her knees in the dark, in the cemetery in Sceaux, throwing up, and she knew that it would never happen like that. Someone else's body, an old man's body, covered her beloved so that she would never be able to rest at his side. And that was the punishment for her, the sinner. She felt herself shaking all over; it was raining harder now. She whispered *Pierre Pierre Pierre* in a low voice, but he did not come to her aid, he was silent. No Benefactor. Not even Blanche to cry with. She was absolutely and utterly forsaken, she was on her knees in the mud of a dark cemetery in a hostile world that would never forgive her; her beloved Pierre was dead, she would never be able to rest at his side; Blanche could give her no solace or guidance; Marie was ultimately alone, she hadn't heard a word from Paul, *had she left his side,* he too was shattered but he would rise again, wounded but not annihilated, but for her it was all over. The fall was complete, from the highest heights into the deepest darkness of the sea.

If only she could die, but there were the children, after all.

She was so cold that she couldn't think. The gravestone seemed vast and menacing, not protective; still no signals, still no messages from Pierre. Why should he answer her? Perhaps he knew what had happened.

She had to go back.

Amor Omnia Vincit, Blanche used to tell her. It was raining harder. She stood up, she left, she rushed home, crouching low, taking short short steps, heading toward what perhaps could get no worse. This was the lowest possible point, she thought with a sense of hope.

But she couldn't be sure.

She returned, an hour after midnight, to the children who had finally, mercifully fallen asleep.

6.

She was awakened around ten when a window shattered. Someone had thrown a rock through the window.

Shouting. She realized what they were shouting, it was the same as before: *the foreign whore*. Quickly she herded the children into the kitchen, because the windows did not face the street. She gave them something to eat and cleaned up the shards of glass.

She managed to get a phone message through.

Around three in the afternoon Marguerite Borel arrived from Paris—she would later recall in her memoirs that she was "shaking with fury"—along with André Debierne to rescue Marie and the children from Sceaux; they had received a cry for help from the desperate Marie, who feared for the lives of her children. People had gathered outside her house and were shouting "Out with the whore" or "Out with the foreigner who stole a married man."

It was quite true that the house was practically besieged, but no one had yet tried to force entry. A few curses were heard when the two friends arrived, but the crowds gave way for their coach. They went inside. Marie was sitting in the kitchen with a child on either side of her. They were holding her hands. Marie's face was ashen and looked suddenly very old; her clothing was sullied with what looked like dried mud.

Marguerite recalled that ten days earlier Marie had been awarded the Nobel Prize in chemistry, but she didn't want to say anything.

You have to leave, was all they said to her. She didn't reply but obeyed.

They managed without incident to make their way through the besiegers, who in silent loathing watched the Polish woman flee. In the coach back to Paris, Marie sat rigidly, like a stone statue, with her head stubbornly turned toward the window and the passing landscape. They assured her that she and the children would be given safe haven with the Borels, in their apartment.

Finally they arrived. Silently, white in the face and with

rigid dignity, she walked across the courtyard and into her new prison.

Three days later, late at night and under the cover of darkness, she went to her own apartment to find out how things were going for Blanche.

I've been anxiously waiting, was the first thing that Blanche said, because I was beside myself with worry for you, Marie. As for me, I'm fine.

There was plenty of food.

They wept together for a long time; Marie picked up Blanche and sat holding her in her arms, as if Blanche were a lost dog that had been found, and whose warmth was comforting.

They had a great deal to talk about.

It was rumored that Paul had been involved in a duel with a journalist; they had fired into the air, and the whole thing had been ridiculous, but the honor of both duelists had been upheld. The Minister of Education had summoned Émile Borel, who was a teacher at École normale, and issued a reprimand for opening his home, which was located in an annex of the school, to someone who was a disgrace to the school. The minister had been extraordinarily indignant, demanding that Borel throw Marie out of his apartment and threatening him with a demotion. But Borel had steadfastly refused to expel Marie. Marguerite Borel's father had also intervened, demanding that his daughter distance herself from this scandal: "Scandals rub off like oil"; but Marguerite had also refused. Yet it was known, her father had reported, that within a few days the ministerial council was going to discuss the case, and a proposal had been made urging Marie Skłodowska to leave the country. Marie could undoubtedly find a teaching position, possibly a professorship, in Poland. After a long argument, Marguerite's father had furiously thrown one of his shoes at the door.

Nothing was pure, everything was ridiculous.

Marie rocked Blanche in her arms. They sat like that all night. When dawn came, Blanche was asleep, and Marie put her to bed; Blanche was so light, after all, like a child.

Then she started going through the mail.

There was a letter from Sweden, from Svante Arrhenius, a board member of the Royal Academy of Science, which a few weeks earlier had awarded her the Nobel Prize in chemistry, her second Nobel Prize, although this time awarded to her alone.

The tone of the letter was cold, in contrast to the previous correspondence.

"*A letter alleged to be yours was published in a French daily newspaper and copies have also been circulating here. As a result, I have consulted my colleagues as to how we ought to react to the situation that has arisen. Everything indicates, falsely I hope, that the published correspondence is not a pure fabrication.*

All of my colleagues replied that it would be desirable if you did not make an appearance here on December 10. Consequently, I request that you remain in France; no one can know with certainty what might happen during the prize ceremony.

If the academy believed that the letter in question might be authentic, it would not—in all likelihood—have awarded the prize to you until you had presented a credible assurance that the letter had been falsified.

It is therefore my hope that you will send a telegram to the permanent secretary C. Aurivillius or to me stating that you have been prevented from attending, and that you then write a letter saying that you will not accept the prize until it can be proven that the accusations against you are completely groundless."

The Swedes didn't want her either.

That's how far things had gone. That's how things had developed.

She woke Blanche and read the letter aloud, in its entirety, in a very clear, almost childish voice.

They don't want me anymore, she then said after a long silence. *The Swedes don't want me. They want me to give up the prize voluntarily, out of shame.*

"And what are you thinking of doing?" asked Blanche.

Marie didn't reply, merely went out to the kitchen and prepared a light breakfast for both of them from what she could find in the pantry. Then Blanche talked to her for a long time, and according to her own words in the Book of Questions, in an almost uncontrolled and at any rate unprintable fashion, commenting on those *Swedish whoremongers and asses* of the Royal Academy of Science who had the gall to criticize her friend.

"I've done nothing reprehensible," Marie then whispered, almost inaudibly, as if testing to see if the words were true.

I've done nothing reprehensible.

"Then send that as your answer," Blanche retorted. And that's what Marie did, in a letter to academy member Gösta Mittag-Leffler, in which she pointed out that the prize had been awarded to her for her discovery of radium and polonium, and that she intended to accept this prize, and at the prearranged place, on December 10 in the year of our Lord 1911.

And that's what happened.

She arrived in Stockholm on the morning of December 10 in a gray drizzle, and that evening she received the prize from the hands of King Gustav V. At the ceremony she carried herself with a stiff and terror-stricken dignity; it was noted that her face was gray and that she seemed exhausted and ill. She wore, according to *Svenska Dagbladet,* "what one is tempted to call an intentionally simple black gown without any sort of adornment." No mud. When she received the prize "the applause took on the character of an ovation." According to *Dagens Nyheter,* she thanked the king with "a slight courtly bow."

She had steeled herself, *and not for one second did I allow myself to be affected by the whispering or insinuations.*

The newspapers kept silent, if they even knew. She permitted only one interview, during which she sat holding the hand of her daughter Irène, who had accompanied her to Stockholm. That was at the Grand Hôtel. The newspapers treated her like a queen. Time after time she said she was ill and exhausted, and that's why there was only one interview. On the same day of the prize ceremony, December 10, *Dagens Nyheter* ran a full-page report on the British situation, meaning the struggle for a woman's right to vote, and, in particular, on the so-called suffragette battle of November 21, written by the journalist Elin Wägner. It had been bloody. Asked about this current issue, Marie replied that she "naturally was a feminist," but unfortunately, because of her research, she had not had time to devote herself to the political struggle. Her daughter was described as sweet and likable. Everyone was concerned about Marie's health; she was described as fragile. Once a smile passed over her face; it was magical. Mittag-Leffler gave the congratulatory speech with unwavering composure. In her Nobel speech, Marie presented a survey of the fifteen-year history of radioactivity. She paid tribute to her husband Pierre, but also emphasized that the results of her research were hers alone, and it was for these results that the prize had been awarded to her.

In the newspapers not a word about the storm in Paris. One evening Marie was the guest of honor at a dinner for three hundred women who were involved in the fight for suffrage. Marie, after all, had been awarded two of the four Nobel Prizes that had so far gone to women; the others were Bertha von Suttner and Selma Lagerlöf. For three hours she was enveloped by their warmth; *if only I could have remained in that state, free from shame.*

Then she returned to Paris, and almost immediately she fell

ill. The brief winter week in Stockholm had been liberatingly cold and pure, but purity was not to be hers. She had only a brief moment of hard-won strength, *I will fight back*, a winter week in Stockholm, *stand up on your legs and walk*, and with almost incomprehensible strength she had actually stood up on her legs and walked. But nothing, absolutely nothing had changed in that hell to which she now had to return, and there the anxiously waiting Blanche, the torso in the wooden box, was the only one who could offer solace, because she may have learned part of the secret of love, if such a thing existed, but it might exist, it might, oh, if only it did.

7.

She began her flight in December 1911; it would last almost three years.

On December 29 she was admitted to a hospital. A number of radiation ulcerations were diagnosed around her uterus, kidneys, and ureter; they were characterized as old and in most cases healed. In January she was very weak, and she wrote her will, in which she distributed the radium that was in her possession. She lost weight and in March was operated on by Doctor Charles Walther, who removed the painful and troublesome lesions.

In letters to Blanche, she notes with humor that her own amputations had now begun, predicting that both of them would end up as very tiny miniatures, sharing a wooden box.

She weighs 51 kilos. In spite of her attempts to conceal where she is, the French press has now gotten wind of her precarious condition and hints that she is in the hospital because Paul Langevin has made her pregnant and that she may have undergone, although it's not certain, an abortion. Possibly with unfortunate complications. Or that she intends to give birth in secret.

Her doctors then publish a strong denial in *Le Temps*. It makes no difference. She can see no way out.

At the end of March she travels to a little town by the name of Brunoy under the pseudonym of Madame Dłuska. Her children come to visit. Marie finds the shame unbearable, but she accepts it because she still claims her right to love. In June she is sent to Thonon-les-Bains, at the foot of the French Alps, to undergo a hydrotherapeutic treatment in the mineral springs, which are supposed to help against pyelonephritis.

Where is her lover?

She feels a dull ache in her Fallopian tubes that lasts from two in the morning until the afternoon, when the pain lessens somewhat. She calls herself Madame Skłodowska and implores everyone to keep her place of refuge secret.

Marie, Marie, it will never end.

In May a letter reaches her from her English friend Hertha Ayrton, inviting her to escape to England. She decides to make the trip. Hertha Ayrton is a physicist and suffragette; Marie is said to be someone who has devoted her whole life to science. Poland was her political world, otherwise nothing.

Suddenly a jolt through the earth's surface, an earthquake? has something happened? then calm returns. Utter calm.

Hertha had been in despair on Marie's behalf. You need protection, and peace and quiet, she wrote.

Peace and quiet? Even though the struggle for suffrage was at its height of violence, maybe it would be possible to find an eye in the storm in London.

Hertha Ayrton was an internationally famous physicist who had made major contributions within the field of electromagnetic wave motion and wave phenomena in oscillating water. During the First World War her research also found a practical use, when her invention, *the Ayrton Fan*, contributed to improving the dissipation of incoming poison gas in the trenches. She was one of the leaders of the British suffragette movement, which was then in the midst of the most brutal phase of the battle for a woman's right to vote. It's true that Marie had signed a proclamation in support of the imprisoned and hunger-striking suffragettes in London, but she was now merely a scandal-shrouded refugee who wanted to hide her shame.

She went to England to find peace and quiet; she landed in the middle of a storm.

Blanche concludes The Black Book with these summer months of 1912.

Marie also writes; she writes a letter to Blanche with the peculiar statement: *I now have an excellent hiding place because I find myself in a storm in which everything is more important than Marie Curie.* She writes the letter from Hertha Ayrton's apartment, which served as a place of refuge for suffragettes who had been on a hunger strike in prison for such a long time that they were near death; they had then been released, for political reasons, to be fattened up so they could once again be imprisoned.

I don't think they dare imprison our foremost leader, Mrs. Pankhurst, she wrote. *She is emaciated, near death, and in a radiant mood, lying on a mattress along with three other comrades in Hertha's library. This is a war. Hertha fattens them up, and when they regain their strength, the next militant action awaits them. They go out in groups with a maximum of twelve people because the law is such that larger groups are not permitted. This group demonstrates at the legally permitted distance from the next group, meaning with at least fifty meters between them, and between the next and the next. These women are often more than seventy years old and physically frail, and yet they are treated with unusual brutality by the police, and imprisoned. In prison they again protest by staging a hunger strike, only to be released, before death sets in, by merciful politicians who would rather have them die outside of prison than inside. Then they are revived by their comrades.*

Hertha's daughter Barbara, one of the women most wanted by the police, fled to France in the spring, disguised in such long and modest clothing that the police couldn't possibly suspect her of being a suffragette. But now she's back in prison. Everyone here has been terribly mistreated by the police, but they're all in good spirits. Two policemen are posted at the front door, and two at the back. The women are carried in and out on stretchers, mostly in.

They can go out under their own power, whether on their way to demonstrations, to prison, or to a hunger strike.

A taxi is always waiting on the street, in case Mrs. Pankhurst should take it into her head to climb up onto the roof and try to flee: then the police are supposed to track her down in the taxi. But since she can hardly walk, there seems little risk of that.

The events of the last six months seem unreal. I think of you, Blanche, every day. Hertha says that I need to put on weight. She seems to have given up her work as a physicist and now her sole purpose is to fatten up her dying comrades; and I, to my great surprise, am counted among them. She plans to take me away from this house on Norfolk Square to Highcliff, by the sea.

No one recognizes me. George Eliot once lived here. I find myself in the midst of chaos. I haven't thought about the word "shame" for a week.

In the eye of the hurricane, cheerfully calm. Marie is confused, she says in letter after letter. This desiccated and cheerful Mrs. Pankhurst! to whom Marie feeds gruel with a spoon!

Was that how comical life could be?

They actually did go to the sea. Hertha must have seen that Marie was very near the precipice. Marie incognito, as usual.

They went to Highcliff in August, and stayed for two months.

8.

She had always loved the solitude near the sea.

She could take long walks on the shore, no longer as weak as she had been in the spring after her operation. She took very

small steps so as not to reawaken the pain in her abdomen. I tot-
ter around like an old woman, she thought, cut.

How long ago was it that she was a woman? She remembers lying naked on a bed in Paris, and the door opened and a
key rattled; it was dark, the lights from the street struck the ceiling, a pause on the way to Nome, no fear; why did it go wrong?
She lay next to him and there was no tomorrow, that word!
tomorrow! What was that poem he had read to her? *Now we lie
utterly still / your shadow has released its grip / we have forgotten those
who did us harm / and there is no tomorrow*—no, was she the one
who read it? She couldn't remember.

It was the first verse of a Polish poem. So she must have
been the one who read it.

Dark in the room. No tomorrow. That's exactly the way it
was, those brief moments when it was best.

Was it only two years ago?

She had been an almost young, almost beautiful woman and
not afraid of anything, and she had made him strong.

And now.

For a few brief months she had found herself in a female
chaos where almost no one knew her, or at any rate no one
knew of the shame; and it was as if she could breathe again. She
was not alone. She had actually never asked herself the question
what is the meaning of it all? It had always been obvious. Now it
was no longer obvious.

Mrs. Pankhurst had *giggled as she lapped up the gruel*, at death's
door! Marie couldn't get over it.

The storm on the Channel coast was not ingratiating and
gentle and friendly but matter-of-fact, and it asked different
questions; that was as it should be. The rain that was falling harder and harder painfully struck her face. This coast was not ingratiating. She liked it. The storm blew hard, a slanting rainstorm

from the east, and she took short short steps along the rocky shore, and she thought: here is a very old woman taking tiny steps, but she's walking.

It's almost a miracle, she's walking.

The first week in September was very beautiful and quiet. She and Hertha sat under the chestnut tree, and then Hertha said that she wasn't sure that she had done the right thing. She had abandoned her research for politics, but perhaps she ought to have done the same as Marie.

Devoted everything to science. Then she might have done greater good.

Marie did not reply. It was absurd. A life in the service of research! And then to doubt!

At the end of September the autumn storms came in quick succession.

She was sleeping better now, the pain had eased, appearing only between four and six in the morning. Marie had asked Hertha how she happened to become a suffragette. What was the actual starting point? What had prompted it? And then Hertha had told her about when she was seventeen and read the Bible.

The Old Testament—she was a Jewess—and the Book of Esther.

It was the first chapter, which tells of the feast of King Ahasuerus. It was this Ahasuerus who ruled from India as far as Ethiopia, over one hundred twenty-seven provinces. And he gave a banquet for all his princes and servants, and the banquet lasted for a hundred and eighty days. At the same time Vashti, the queen, also gave a banquet for the women in King Ahasuerus's royal palace. Then on the seventh day, when the king's heart was merry with wine, he commanded Mehuman, Biztha, Harbona, Bigtha, Abagtha, Zethar, and Carkas, the seven chamberlains, to bring Queen Vashti, wearing only the royal crown, before the king so that he might let the people and the princes see her beauty, for she was fair to behold.

But Queen Vashti refused to come. The king then grew angry and asked the men who were versed in law and judgment what he should do. And they said to him: "Queen Vashti has done wrong not only to the king but to all the princes and all the people in all of King Ahasuerus's provinces. For what the queen has done will become known among all the women, and will cause them to have contempt for their husbands, since they will then be able to say: 'King Ahasuerus commanded Queen Vashti to be brought before him, but she did not come.'"

And that was the end of Queen Vashti.

And Hertha, whose name was Phoebe Sarah before she changed her name to Hertha since she was a Jewess, thought it was so unfair. Vashti was a role model. And Hertha had been furious.

Was that simply how it was? Was that how life was? That a person was struck, like a billiard ball with a stick? Just like that?

Yes, just like that. Haven't you ever been struck, Marie? she asked.

Only by the blue light, she replied.

A letter from Blanche reached Marie Skłodowska, as she now called herself in the tenth month of her flight.

She read it in solitude, at the shore, and wept.

The last week of September she went back to Paris.

She had a question to ask Blanche and knew that she had to hurry, time was short. Perhaps she would receive an answer.

On October 2 she entered Blanche's room. Blanche was sitting in the wooden box. She had been well taken care of, but she couldn't help crying.

She had been so filled with longing, and now Marie was back.

That night Marie was able to ask the important question, which in the eternity of eternities would never have an answer but still had to be asked, and she asked it, and in The Red Book Blanche left an answer. It was the only answer she could give, that was why the story had to be told; that's how it was, that's how it happened, that was the whole story.

The Red Book

V I I I

THE SONG OF THE BLUE LIGHT

1.

INCREASINGLY FILLED WITH ANGUISH ON MARIE'S BEHALF.

The night before she fled, Marie asked me what the *innermost secret* of love was. It was all so ugly! It was also so painful: those brief moments of dizziness, and then all that ugliness in the wake of love! What had I said to Charcot? she asked me. Had I said something that made him understand?

"Once when he was crying," I then replied to my own surprise and without thinking, "I said '*I'll never leave your side.*'"

"Was that all?" she then asked.

But that *was* all.

I know. I don't have much time left.

I write with the only hand I have, but that too will soon be taken from me. Marie often asks me if she should feel guilty for this disease, if the radiation from the radium is the cause; I don't want her to feel guilty and then take pity on me. I want her to do it out of love for me. That's why I mention my two years as an assistant in Salpêtrière's x-ray department before she met me.

Who knows whether my diminution is due to Professor Röntgen or to pitchblende?

She is my only friend. If I didn't exist, she would be dead; I'm keeping both of us alive with my amputated stories about love in the new century.

Yet I fear that I can no longer explain the nature of love. Nor the love between me and Charcot. *I'll never leave your side*— I didn't tell Marie the context, but I remember the situation well.

It was the first or second week of March in 1891. Charcot had suffered his first extremely painful heart attack. It was at a dinner, two and a half years before his death. And incidentally, Louis Pasteur happened to be present. Charcot suddenly felt a strong and painful contraction in the area of his heart, and he turned deathly pale. Doctor Viguir raced off to get a certain Professor Potain, who lived only a block away. It was late, so he opened the door wearing his nightshirt, but quickly dressed. After an hour and some medical treatment, the pains eased. The following day Charcot came to see me—I was then in the laundry section of the hospital. We went into the ironing room and I ordered the two women who were working there to leave the room.

His message was very brief.

"Two and a half years," he said. "That's all the time I have left." And then he started to cry.

"*I'll never leave your side,*" I then told him.

That was when he ought to have understood. *I'll never leave your side.* But if the nature of love can only be described in this way, then everything I've written in order to save Marie may be basically meaningless. I realize that I'll never be able to get any farther.

That's a relief. But I feel sorry for Marie.

She was hoping, after all, with my guidance to make sense of it all, so that she could finally say: *that's how it was, that's how it happened, that was the whole story.* And I hope that she still thinks so.

2.

I don't have much time left.

I'm going to refrain from asking any introductory questions in this section of the Book of Questions—the part that I call The Red Book because it carries the red color of love. I once wanted to write it as if the story were a conversation between two people.

But I'm all alone. Everyone is.

What happened on the journey to Morvan, what I at Marie's insistent urging told her about when she returned from England and was at her wits' end, it's much too painful and yet also filled with joy.

But I have very little time.

Many people have sought me out to ask me to testify about my days at Salpêtrière, about Charcot, about the Friday lectures, about my role in them, and about his last days and death. But why do they ask me? Many have testified about the lot of the women at Salpêtrière. Most recently a meddlesome man by the name of Baudoin: He wanted testimony confirming that the whole thing was a deception, but he didn't get it.

Everyone seems to have seen me, no one seems to have seen me.

But about the very end there is no written documentation, nothing about the last days, about the journey to Morvan, or about Charcot's final hours. No, I'm wrong, one account does exist. I've read it, by a certain René Vallery-Radot, the son-in-law of Louis Pasteur. He was not along on the journey to Morvan, but he seems to have talked to those two weasels. I know him well, an opportunist who, out of consideration for Charcot's memory, says not one word about me going along on the journey, nor does he say anything about my role in saving Charcot's life.

It doesn't matter to me. I'm going to die soon myself. Death will diminish me, just as the amputations have diminished my body. Death will diminish me, but also my ambitions, my pride.

What happiness was, that's something you decide after the fact.

I've decided to call the relationship between Jean Martin Charcot and myself *the story of a classic loving couple*. It makes the love easier to bear. If the pain is heightened, it becomes formidable and yet bearable because in some sense it becomes historic. I've said as much to Marie. She then looks at me with astonishment. I understand her. This cut torso in its wooden box on wheels is perhaps not a symbol for eternal love.

A classic loving couple. Everyone ought to think that way. You can transform yourself into a classic loving couple. Marie ought to do it. Marie and Pierre. Marie and Paul. Blanche and Charcot.

I could never address him by his first name.

Why did he take me along on the journey?

Everyone knew that he was married and had three children and respected and feared his wife, and no one knew about my role. I think everyone regarded me as the beautiful Blanche whom no one, especially Charcot, was allowed to touch; the powerless and deadly woman. It was the combination of desire and death that enticed them. Everyone felt desire, no one was allowed to touch, everyone knew that I could kill, which increased their desire, and protected me. I was known for this. It was my foremost talent. Charcot knew better. I want you to come along, he said, I'm ill, I'm in pain, angina pectoris, I know that I'm going to die, I want you to come along.

And so we began the journey to Morvan.

I didn't want anyone to be afraid of me.

Why did they force me? It's not fair.

Sometimes I think that if we put all our loves together, I mean my loves and Marie's, then an image of life itself would emerge, in the spaces in between. My life, and Marie's.

Marie has had the same thought. Sometimes she asks me if I'm envious of her. Then I stare at her in silence. But I assume that she's thinking about Salpêtrière, and comparing. That's when I say the line about the *classic loving couple*.

Then Marie usually laughs. That's how the days and nights pass.

It's possible to imagine a love that was solely wrapped up in itself. That's what I often think about in moments of desperation and melancholy. As if a glass bell were tipped over on top of life. Maybe that would make it less painful. Why do you love animals more than people? I once asked Charcot. He got upset and denied it. Do you love me more than a dog? I then said.

I wanted to hurt him, in order to make him understand. Blanche, he said, you are absurdly strong, and I'm afraid of you. But you shouldn't exploit the weakness of the one who loves you more than he loves life.

Then how much did he love life? I don't know. We went to Morvan.

3.

There were four of us who got on the train at Gare de Lyon.

Two of them I hadn't met before. Professor Debove and

Professor Straus also greeted me with a certain respect, although it was not as reverential as their respect for Charcot.

Why this journey! they asked their master. But no reply.

It wasn't until later that I understood why Charcot undertook this journey: he wanted to revisit his youth. I didn't know that he had spent many years in this landscape, and especially in the town of Vézelay. What are you looking for? I asked. Why does a person seek out his youth? he asked me in turn. I replied *it's what a person does in the moment right before he gives up*, whereupon our two companions regarded me with indignation and astonishment. To distract the two loathsome weasels sitting across from us in the compartment during the two-hour train trip, I conversed with Charcot. He had once told me about an incident at Saint-Malo when his brother found himself in the utmost danger; I asked about his brother's well-being today. He looked at me with a sudden and surprising expression of fury, in silence, but a few minutes later he replied: *a person seeks out his youth because everything has to make sense!*

A bridge, the train very slowly crossing the river. *In a river like this I bade farewell to my mother!* I noted with a gentle smile at my friend, *that's how it makes sense!*

I didn't mean him any harm. I was merely trying to reach him.

We made a brief stop at Château de Bussy, for fourteen years a prison for the author de Bussy, imprisoned by Louis XIV because of his offensive writings. De Bussy had painted clumsy pictures on the walls, the work of an amateur; Charcot remarked that imprisoned artists often display peculiar similarities to hysterical or spastic patients. His two colleagues wrote down this comment. Does that mean that I'm an artist? I asked. Do you draw grotesque figures on the walls? he retorted with an odd smile. My inner walls are covered, I have inscribed drawings by using a nail. Why a nail? he asked. Because art has to hurt, I replied. He laughed softly; his two companions, Professor

Debove and Professor Straus, laughed heartily. That was the end of our field trip to the castle of the author de Bussy.

I'm trying to reach inside of him. I don't have much time, he doesn't have much time. That's how things can turn out. A whole lifetime of hesitating, and then suddenly everything has to be said.

On the third day we reached Vézelay; *this looks like Perugia or Siena*, remarked Charcot, explaining that when he was a young doctor he had spent a considerable amount of time there. His companions, the professors Debove and Straus, wrote down this comment. We walked up to the cathedral, I held his arm. For a moment it seemed to me that we were both young medical students and that I could hold his hand, but the two weasel-like academics who were following close behind, at a distance of two or three meters, made this impossible or at least very difficult.

Blanche, he said in a low voice, let's go inside the cathedral, it's empty. My beloved, I replied in a low voice (and this was the first time I used this expression; I must have been very tired or over-excited), I will follow you wherever you like.

We went inside.

Charcot pointed out to me the *narthex*, the place for the catechumens, and the rectangular hole in the basilica wall, which was the place for the impoverished and insane; *those who are possessed shout from the walls and no one helps them*, he said with an oddly sorrowful smile. From this place, this hole in the mighty stone wall, the possessed could and must listen and from the altar obedience was drummed into them, yet they were not permitted to see the altar, which was much too holy for them. *This basilica is in that sense like our auditorium at Salpêtrière, where those who are possessed sing their songs of sorrow!* I turned around after this remark by Charcot, smiling, as I thought, at the two weasels and told them to write down that Professor Charcot was an altar. They gave a forced laugh.

I didn't mean to be cruel.

I knew that something was wrong, that something was about to happen; I was frightened. These walls are terrifying and thick, like those in a citadel or a prison, Charcot noted, you can hear shouts coming from these walls: "*misfortune will strike those who are without faith.*" I asked him whether he was tired and would like to rest; he said yes and pointed at a bench to the left of the *portico*. Then we sat down, and he wanted to hold my hand. *What have I created during my life, tell me that, Blanche, have I created a basilica like this one, for lunatics, or a sect for those who need faith?* The two weasels with their notebooks seemed bewildered. With a wave of his hand Charcot directed them to a bench about twenty feet away from us; they sat down with gestures of despair. Blanche, whispered Charcot, his face nearly expression-less, *there is so much that you haven't said and I don't know; what do I know about you except that I love you and you push me away?*

How well I remember his face. The rigid shell that was about to shatter, and his despair. Then he said, in the same pre-cise and calm voice, *I've reached the conclusion that the direction of my research regarding hysteria and neurological disturbances in women in recent years has been utterly flawed, my concept of hysteria now seems decadent, all my assumptions about the pathology of the nervous system have to be revised, it's necessary to start over from the very beginning.*

The two weasels, Professor Debove and Professor Straus, leaned forward with the same expression of breathless despair they had displayed a moment ago; they couldn't hear what their master was saying, they were not taking notes.

I alone could hear.

To me he said in that cathedral in Vézelay that he loved me, that I had been burned into him like a branding iron on an innocent animal, that I had pushed him away, that this was about to kill him, that his time would soon be up, that everything had been meaningless, including his research, and that he now had to start over from the beginning; and none of this was written down by the two observers, I'm referring here to the professors

Debove and Straus, the two weasels. He told me that only to his private secretary, Georges Guinon, had he mentioned his return to zero, and that everything had been a failure.

I was in all respects alone with him, with my despair, my wish to make sense of things, to understand his love, my guilt, and why this journey to Morvan would mean his death and my liberation.

4.

We left Vézelay on the morning of August 14, 1893.

We drove out of the city, we passed a graveyard; Charcot merely remarked, in Italian, *Campo santo*. He talked about a book by Guy de Maupassant that he had read the previous night, *it's so sad, it's the work of a sick person, the world is not as evil as he describes, goodness does exist*. The professors Debove and Straus wrote down these words. And when asked by one of these attentive hyenas of his whether his faith in God was unwavering, he merely shook his head sadly and replied *if he exists, he is far, far away, and so vague, so hazy*.

They wrote everything down, except for what I said. They seemed to be afraid of me.

As we were leaving the hotel in Vézelay, a man came over to us, seized Charcot's hand, kissed it, and explained that he had been Charcot's patient but was now well; he was an artist and wanted to thank him. This made a loathsome impression on me: like something out of the Bible, a lamb that could walk and was thanking his Savior. I told this to Charcot in a scornful voice; he was no Jesus Christ, after all! He flinched, as if he'd been struck, and merely nodded.

The two vultures muttered indignantly.

Charcot sat beside me in the landau, occasionally holding my hand, in spite of the fact that the professors Debove and Straus were sitting across from us, looking at us with deference

and indignation. I asked them whether they had ever seen a performance with me; they both replied affirmatively (nodding
almost simultaneously)—I then asked what their impression had
been. Professor Debove replied that he had been so preoccupied
with writing down Professor Charcot's comments, which were
of such great and unique scientific value, that he had hardly
raised his eyes and thus didn't want to comment on me or my
role in the events. Hypocrite, I retorted in a friendly voice; they
didn't write down this remark. I turned around, saw a smile pass
swiftly over Charcot's lips. We rode across a bridge. In the past
there was only a ferry.

It spanned the Cure River. I took a deep breath.

We arrived at Auberge des Settons around 4:30 in the afternoon.

Because Charcot had never been religious—on the contrary, during periods of his life he had been *intolerant*—he spoke
at dinner on the topics of archaeology, history, the fine arts, and
botany. What should we do? I asked him directly, completely
ignoring the two scribes who were sitting at our table. Charcot
then ordered the two professors Debove and Straus to take an
evening stroll around the lake. They bowed their assent and
withdrew; I knew they could have killed me.

That was the last evening. That's how it began.

Charcot's room at the inn Auberge des Settons was simply
furnished, with a table, two chairs, a water pitcher, a basin, something that I took to be a washcloth, a bed. I had often imagined
a place called a *chambre d'amour* that would be purer, not so worn
out, maybe not a bigger room, but bigger in feeling, purer! Such
a room would be vaguely furnished, maybe with a bed, maybe
with a canopy; I imagined some sort of light but without a light

source, or a darkness that did not shut out the two lovers from each other.

Charcot asked me to come to his room. I went in.

He was sitting on the bed, his back bowed, he was looking down at the floor, he didn't speak.

I asked him if he was in pain. He merely shook his head.

Dusk had fallen outside. I opened a door to a closet, hung up his clothes, found a candlestick and a candle. Don't light it, he said; I lit it, put the candle on the table. In a low voice he began talking about the memories he had of Salpêtrière, mentioned someone by the name of Jane Avril, he didn't think I would remember her, talked about the young girl by the name of Jane Avril who had arranged, or participated in, a dance performance, a Danse des Fous, that became transformed into something *existential*. She had suddenly freed herself from gravity and history and filth, *as if a miracle were possible*. He had, when he saw her, been seized with something that felt like dizziness. And during the dance, as peculiar steps and movements seemed to be born out of nothing, she had suddenly emerged as the image of a human being freed from her shackles, freed from her assumptions. As if she were not a machine at all but understood that a person could choose her own life, and dance into a new one.

As if she were *a butterfly that had escaped from heaven*, I then interjected.

He looked up at me in surprise. I knew her well, I told him. Of course I knew Jane Avril. And I remember the dance. At the time I whispered to her that she danced as if she were a butterfly that had escaped from heaven, that had been frightened, and wanted to play with us. I could have wept, or killed her; then she disappeared. Was that my fault?

Where did she go? Charcot asked.

Where do they go, all those butterflies that are freed? I don't know, no doubt they flutter back to their cages, I replied. A butterfly doesn't live in a cage, retorted Charcot. I've heard that she's still dancing, I replied, I suppose she's trying to remember and find her way back; I'm afraid that the dance has become petrified, is no longer that of a butterfly. Find her way back to what? he asked. To that brief moment when anything was possible, and before she knew better.

Maybe it's like love.

I stood at the window with my back to him, he was still sitting on the bed. It was dark outside. I imagined the two scribes wandering around the lake like two gnomes; I couldn't see them, couldn't see the lake or Professor Debove or Professor Straus. I'm not in pain, I heard him say from the dim light of the room, as if to himself. He was still sitting on his bed with his arms hanging limply.

Good, was the only thing I could say.

But I don't have much time, he said then in such a low voice that I almost didn't hear him.

Why did you bring me along? I asked.

Why did you come? he said.

5.

I had set the single candle on a table at the foot of the bed; it flickered, it was now pitch-dark outside.

The darkness in the room was also flickering; we shared this darkness. His face was white and anxious, he repeated that he wasn't in any pain, at the same time he pressed his hand to his chest, he was frightened. I helped him get undressed, I removed his clothing from above the waist, leaned him back against the pillow; he was breathing with his mouth open. His skin was smooth and soft like a child's. With my fingers I combed his hair, which was in disarray, and I loosened his belt so that he could breathe easier. The room was hot, almost suffocatingly hot, I opened a window slightly.

I'm not in pain, he repeated again, like an invocation.

Don't be afraid, I said.

Why shouldn't I be afraid? he whispered, I know that there isn't much time, I don't have much time, then it's black, nothing. Like sleep, I whispered back, running my hand soothingly through his hair. No, it won't be at all like sleep, I know that; when I'm asleep I'm surrounded by dreams, then I'm not alone, it's a darkness inhabited by creatures, sometimes dancing figures; when I wake up, I often remember them. But I'm never alone when I dream. When I'm dead, I won't be able to seek solace in dreams, there is no dancing darkness.

Not even a dancing butterfly? I whispered.

Not even that! no hazy dancing figures. I know there won't be any Blanche coming toward me and smiling and touching me with her hand and stroking my cheek. When I'm dead it will be black and dreamless. That's what terrifies me. That you won't be able to dream about me anymore? Yes, that too. And everything that is now too late! that you will disappear into the dark, having never really existed. Although you were so close to existing. The fact that I've lived an entire lifetime next to you, day and night, and that it's only in dreams that you touched me, and now I stand near a precipice and there everything is black.

No Blanche?

No Blanche, nothing.

I stood up, closed the window. It might have been midnight by then, not a sound from the wind through the trees. No voices. The gnomes had surely returned and were sleeping their bitter sleep. It was just the two of us. He was afraid. I wished that I could take him in my arms and lift him up, like a puppy, and reassure him. I knew that I loved him, I knew that he was going to die. What do you do with a beloved who's going to die when an entire lifetime has passed, and you haven't done what you could have done? I heard how he was breathing, labored, his bare torso seemed huge and white; he had no hair on his chest, he was as smooth as a child. What is the answer? he whispered. What should I say? I thought you had the answer to everything, I said. When you stood in the Auditorium and spoke, you had answers. What has happened?

He didn't reply.

I turned around, left the window, which no longer served as an excuse not to look at him. I didn't want him to see that I was crying. I always thought your voice was so beautiful, I said close to his ear; when I slipped into unconsciousness or *Gurney's deep state*, or *Azam's* or *Sollier's*, you see, I've learned! then I would still always hear your voice close to me. I wouldn't understand what you were saying, but your voice, it sounded so young, it was like the voice of a young, tanned boy who was standing in water up to his knees. Do you understand? How beautiful it was. I didn't understand what you said, it was unclear, but you were young like in a dream. Like in a dream? he whispered. Yes, like in a dream.

But what if everything turns black? And completely empty? And I can never again take you with me, Blanche, not even like in a dream? I'm so afraid, he whispered, I can't take anything with me. Not you. I'm so afraid that I won't be able to dream about you ever again.

The candle flame was now motionless, burning straight up; he lay with his eyes closed. He looked so childlike. I lay down close to him. I pressed close to his side, I heard he was struggling to breathe. Don't be afraid, I said. I'm here. I will be with you for an eternity of eternities. For an eternity of eternities?

Yes, always. For all time.

How long ago was it that you came to me, Blanche? Sixteen years. And now? How long will you stay, Blanche?

For an eternity of eternities.

I stroked his chest with my hand, lightly, light as a butterfly; do you remember, I whispered, do you remember the points? I touched the points, he was breathing with his mouth open. Here at the throat, you drew the points with a pen, at the hysterogenic zones, here, the collarbone, under the breast. The side. You never dared touch me with your hand. Why didn't you ever dare touch me?

You were holy.

Holy?

Don't move, I whispered. Lie still. I'm not afraid, I dare touch you; you are not holy, I am not holy. And you are not afraid. I moved my hand in gentle, light strokes over his chest, his neck; his breathing was calmer now. Are you still afraid? No, he whispered, I'm not afraid. And you can hear my voice? Yes, he said, I can hear your voice. If you're standing near a precipice, I whispered, and everything is black down below, then you shouldn't stand alone, then I'll stand next to you.

Are you standing next to me?

Yes, it's pitch dark, but we share the darkness, that's what love is, you're not afraid.

I'm not afraid.

That's good, I whispered. I touched the skin on his chest and arms and neck with my hand, his skin was delicate and silky. I heard that he was breathing calmly, the candle wasn't flickering, everything was warm; I stood up.

I took off my clothes.

He was sleeping like a child, didn't see me, I took off my clothes in the glow of the candle. Here I am, naked, I said next to his cheek, don't move, I'm here, don't be afraid. I took off the rest of his clothes. He didn't move. I lay down next to him. Don't move, I said.

But my hand touched him.

He wanted to say something, but I hushed him. Keep still. Quiet. *And I'll never leave your side.*

The candle flame grew smaller, he no longer had his eyes closed, he was not afraid. He looked at me with such intensity, as if he wanted my eyes to burn into him forever, for an eternity of eternities. I touched his body, his sex, he gasped, he was ready, he lay still, I looked down at his face, I slipped him inside of me.

Touch me, I whispered. And then his hand dared touch my back.

I moved slowly. We were both breathing calmly. When it was over I lay for a long time with my cheek pressed to his, and he whispered; I heard his words but didn't understand their meaning, it was like a child who was about to start talking, something very close to a language but not quite there yet. I slipped off of him, lay down next to him.

Are you in pain? I asked. Never again, he replied after a moment; I understood, asked no more questions.

The candle burned out, it was dark, I was still lying at his side, he was holding my hand in his, suddenly I felt his grip tighten. His body arced up from the bed, I saw his face from the side, pain tore open his mouth. Then the arc sank back, the pain vanished, he lay still.

I held my hand over his mouth. I felt nothing, no breath, he was no longer breathing. The pain had disappeared from his face, and from his body, he lay perfectly still.

He looked endearing. Why should I cry? I had promised, after all, never to leave his side. I stayed where I was, lying at his side.

Dawn came. I was holding his hand in mine.

When it was daylight I got dressed, arranged the way he was resting so that his friends and admirers would not take offense, and then I went out to them and said that Professor J. M. Charcot was dead.

We took him in his coffin back to Paris; neither of them spoke to me, it didn't matter.

Why should they speak to me?

His coffin was placed in the chapel at Salpêtrière, and the inmates of the hospital could then, in a procession of mourners, honor him and show their sorrow. Several thousand of the inmates moved slowly past, many of them carried on stretchers.

I brought a chair and sat down next to the coffin, looking at the mourners passing by us. I kept my hand on his coffin so that he would know that I was there and had not broken my promise. Those who were in charge then came over and said that it was unseemly for me to be sitting there.

I didn't move. And then they left me in peace, together with him.

CODA

(STARTING POINTS)

A LIFE-SIZE STATUE WAS ERECTED TO JEAN MARTIN CHARCOT; it was made of bronze, and it stood in front of the entrance to Salpêtrière Hospital; it stood there for a long time. But when the Germans occupied Paris during the Second World War, the need for metal for the war industry was too great: in 1942 the statue was removed by the German occupiers, melted down, and used in the production of light anti-aircraft guns.

Since that time, there has been no statue of Charcot in front of the door to Salpêtrière.

The last meeting of the three women: it was in the spring of 1913, with Jane Avril, Blanche Wittman, and Marie Curie. The other two rolled Blanche outside in her box, placing her on the terrace. Then they brought chairs, sat down next to her, and conversed. Jane asked Marie how she was doing; she smiled and said *yes, well at least now I can keep food down.*

All of them started laughing. They sat outside on the terrace, Marie, Blanche, and Jane, and it was so tranquil and pleasant and they were so fond of each other.

A month later Blanche was dead.

The terrace. The trees. The foliage.

Marie Skłodowska Curie was buried in the cemetery in Sceaux, in the same grave as her husband Pierre.

Pierre's father, Eugène Curie, had died in 1910 and his coffin was placed on top of his son's. Several years later, after a personal crisis, Marie had the grave dug up and Eugène Curie's coffin was moved underneath, because Marie had decided that her coffin should be placed in direct contact with that of her husband Pierre.

She didn't want to have anything between them.

And that's what was done. When Marie died—on July 4, 1934, from aplastic pernicious anemia that had proceeded rapidly and feverishly, in which her bone marrow did not react, probably because of damage from a long-term accumulation of radiation—her coffin was lowered down to Pierre's, in the little cemetery in Sceaux. Her family, along with five friends, were the only ones present at the ceremony, which was strongly criticized by the newspaper *Le Journal,* one of the French newspapers that never forgave her. The simplicity of the funeral was *a sign of Marie Skłodowska Curie's unsurpassed arrogance, which was manifested in the form of a voluntary effacement, of a refusal to accept honors, of an exaggerated humility.*

One of the five was Paul Langevin. Twenty-four years had passed since they made love for the last time. Amor Omnia Vincit, it said on one of the wreaths; it wasn't his, no one knew who had sent it. Blanche had been dead for twenty years. Yet I have decided to believe that it came from her.

No one knows where Blanche is buried.

ACKNOWLEDGMENTS

THIS IS A NOVEL. I HAVE MADE USE OF FACTUAL MATERIAL BUT only in order to write a novel, and for that reason I don't feel the need to list the works that I've used. Yet regarding the Curie material I would like to mention Evelyn Sharp's *Hertha Ayrton*, Marguerite Borel's *A travers deux siècles. Souvenirs et rencontres*, Karin Blanc's *Marie Curie et le Nobel*, and above all Susan Quinn's groundbreaking treatise *Marie Curie—A Life*, in particular for her discussion of the Langevin tragedy. Special thanks to my daughter Jenny Gilbertsson, who researched the extensive Charcot material. Responsibility for the manner in which I used all of these sources in the story of Blanche and Marie is mine alone.

—P.O.E.